AGRO LAND

A Tale of Horror by

DANIEL ARTHUR SMITH

Author of

The Cathari Treasure

AGROLAND

DANIEL ARTHUR SMITH

This book is a work of fiction and any resemblance to persons, living or dead, is purely coincidental. The characters are productions of the author's imagination and used fictitiously.

Edited By
Crystal Watanabe

Also Written by Daniel Arthur Smith

The Cameron Kincaid Adventures
The Cathari Treasure
The Somali Deception

The Literary Fiction Series
The Potter's Daughter
Opening Day: A Short Story

The Horror Series
Agroland

*****

For Susan, Tristan, & Oliver, as all things are.
&
To the Maple Ridge Elementary class of 1980.

*****

ONE

I've seen a lot of ugliness in the world. The evil things men can do, violent things. Things I chose to forget, to wipe clean. I've walked through what was left of a bombed out market, people blown apart, children blown apart. When a buddy of mine had his leg shredded by a roadside bomb, I gathered his boot with his foot still inside. All of those things, all of that war, none of it prepared me for what we found by the fire.

When I left the Marines, I left the war. I joined a civilian firm assigned to babysit a sleepy little agro outfit out in the desert of north Jordan, not far from the Syrian border. We tagged the place Agroland. They were going to make crops grow in the desert, dates and olives, stuff like that. Jobs were scarce and they wanted vets, insurance to make sure no one showed up to spoil the party. So they got us, a mix of Brits and Americans pretending we were still soldiers. The only thing I had to do was patrol a square mile perimeter that never saw much more than sand and dust. Easy money.

Every day, a couple times a day, I walked the little road lining the compound, making sure no one had cut through the fifteen-foot chain link, or tried to climb over the razor wire on top. I never expected to find anyone. The chain link was like a prison fence, as good at keeping people in as keeping them out, and lined up along the inside were waist high reinforced barriers to stop anyone from driving through. No one was getting in.

I was finishing my midday patrol and things were quiet, like every other day. I stopped when I noticed something on the horizon. Gareth was working nearby, and when he saw me lift my binoculars, he wasted no time coming over to compare notes. He was one of the geologists we were babysitting out there, always happy to tell us what was what, like we were school kids, a real stuffed shirt. The Brit couldn't say good morning without sounding like an ass.

He walked up beside me and stood there, mopping his face and forehead with a stained handkerchief. I pretended I couldn't see him to my side. Finally, he said, "You're looking at the ripples rise up on the horizon."

"Yep," I said, didn't lower the binoculars.

He lifted the brim of his hat to mop the moisture matting his hair, and then said, "That, Aker, is a fata morgana, a mirage."

Two tours deep in the Iraqi sandbox taught me the difference between floating castles and what was real. Within a minute, that ripple of tan became a rolling cloud and the first glints of sun bounced off a hazy line skimming the horizon.

"Or maybe not," I said.

Gareth curled his lip and then headed toward the Greenhouse. He didn't see my silly smile.

I shouldn't have been smiling though. That time of day, that cloud should've been an illusion.

I flipped my palm up to check my watch, then tapped my radio. "Are we expecting anybody?"

Gaz answered from the tower. "That's Tak and June."

Gaz was a Brit too, a real good guy. He had served in Afghanistan before signing on.

"They're back early," I told him, course he already knew. "Coming in fast."

He said, "June radioed in. They have a 'situation'." Then there was a pause. "Max said we're goin' on alert, mate."

"Okay," I said. "Switching channels and on my way."

A 'situation' was no good.

Tak and June had toured in Afghanistan too, together. They patrolled Agroland's outer perimeter twice a day. They requested the duty—we all knew why—and like clockwork, they always came back at the last possible minute, and we knew why that was too.

We had some common sense protocols in place and one was to go on alert if a patrol came in early. Alert meant switch the two-ways to the shared channel and then get to our position. Mine was the gate.

Heading over, I kept an eye on the SUV. They were spitting out a big cone cloud of tan dust behind them.

The gate had already been slid aside by the time I got there. Max and Wizard were waiting. Max was the Brit in charge of security. There were all kinds of rumors about where he had served, SAS, more action with the French, some hard-core Special Forces stuff. Even behind his shades, I could tell he wasn't happy. Wizard was standing right next to him. He had been a Marine stateside and had never gotten any farther than North Carolina. He'd served his tour in some Comsat station before coming to Agroland as a signal tech. The two couldn't be more different, like somebody tried to build two soldiers and used most of the works on the first guy and had nothing left for the next. Max was six four with a blonde flat top, his face bronze and leather worn, and over his forearm was an MP5 that he probably slept with. Wizard was a head shorter than everybody else on the security team. His cover was too big for his head, his flak jacket oversized, and the M16 strapped over his shoulder was two sizes off. Next to Max, he looked like some scrawny kid off the playground that had hauled all of his toys out to play.

As the tech, he had to drag out the bomb detection gear whenever a vehicle came in. He could barely hold the long handle of the inspection mirror and the oversized chemical sniffer at the same time.

Max was running through the compound. There were only a few buildings there, all prefabs except the Greenhouse. The Greenhouse was two-thirds glass, the rest was concrete block. All the hydroponics, aquaponics, and plants were in the glass end, the offices, labs, and radio room were on the other. In between were the cafeteria and kitchen. Off the end of the Greenhouse was a prefab metal hangar we used as a garage. The SUV's, tractors, wagons, and the shipping containers with the diesel and natural gas were kept in there. The Powerhouse and the med hut were at the end of the row. A line of little campers we called pods were off to the side, those were for the higher ups. Across the yard were the barracks, one for security and another for the Jordanian workers. There was the tower in the yard and the tool shed out back on the edge of the Agrofield. Next to that, the water hole and the water shed. The water plant was in there, along with drilling and irrigation gear. A lean-to popped out of one side of the shed to shield the hole and attached to the other side of that was the shower and head.

After taking in the compound, Max squinted his eyes up to Gaz in the tower, and then fixed on me. I guess he had finished calculating whatever went on in his head. "June radioed in," he said. "They found somebody alone out there in the desert. Lucas is already in the med hut and Jenner has everyone eyeballed in the Greenhouse."

"They found someone out there?" I asked. "Some Bedouin? That's impossible." We were on the northern edge of the Syrian Desert, out in the middle of nowhere. Nowhere as in no towns, villages, life, nothing.

Max tightened his lower lip against his teeth and then bit it. I could tell he was cooking what I was saying. As if the timer went off in his oven, he dropped his lip down. "A Bedouin would be possible," he said. "We saw a few on camels fifty klicks from here last winter." Then Max shook his head to the side. "June said this guy is a westerner."

For the first time since my duty in Iraq I snapped my spine straight. During the Iraq War, the Syrian Desert was a major supply line for the Iraqi insurgents. That time had passed but the desert was still a key route for smugglers into Syria, where the latest war had broken out. If terrorists hijacked Tak and June on patrol, they could get them to radio in that they had a survivor that needed medical assistance, and then, as soon as the SUV drove into the compound, boom. I dropped my M16 off my shoulder and readied myself.

Max picked up his two-way. "We're on, people," he said.

Gaz, Lucas, and Jenner rattled back in order. "In position."

TWO

    I took my position on the left side of the gate, across from Wizard. Max planted himself between us, and I mean planted himself, his shoulders popped back like he was going into some stance that was going to make him a solid oak. The gate was already open. We were giving them the benefit of the doubt. Then again, if she was rigged to blow, the chain link gate wasn't going to matter much. Inside the SUV, flashes of daylight cut the interior into silhouettes. Twenty meters out, it began to slow and the face of the driver came into view. June was driving. Her face was stone. Her high cheekbones and dark Latino eyes fixed forward. I raised my M16. Somebody was hunched over in the back, tending to someone or something. I figured that had to be Tak.

Tak's real name was Myron. He was a sharp kid from Jamaica, Queens. His tag was Tak because he was a tactical wiz. He was always playing chess with Max. That is, when he wasn't playing around with June. June was from the Bronx, a real wildcat, hot as a jaguar and just as deadly. June and Tak went way back, and then finally hooked up when they hit Agroland.

The SUV slid to a halt a breath in front of Max. He didn't flinch, he didn't gesture, he stood in that oak tree stance. The dust that had been trailing behind raced up around the SUV, and then hovered in front of him before dissipating. Even the dust was intimidated by that guy.

Wizard went right to work with the chemical sniffer. My job was a lot simpler. Keep my weapon ready, eyeball the exterior, and then on signal, the interior. I waited for Wizard's little gizmo to clear and then when he gave me the nod, I stepped up to the vehicle.

I leaned in from the front of the SUV, peering into the open passenger window at an angle. June had opened both windows straight away when she made the gate. The heat from the engine shot at my cheek and the acrid fumes of engine coolant slid under my sunglasses and bit into my eyes. June's hands are still at ten and two, her eyes fixed on the med hut. I held back for a second until Wizard had the inspection mirror under my side of the truck and then I stuck my head in to get a better view of the back. Tak was kneeling over somebody. The stranger's face was hidden behind the seat. I could only make out what was left of his sun bleached clothes and a forearm up against the tailgate. The wrinkled forearm was thin, wooden, and brown like tanned leather. I glanced up at Tak's face. His eyes were wide and his head was bobbing up and down in little short nods.

My eyes darted back to June. "You all right?" I asked her.

June didn't turn her head. Her fingers were drumming

against the steering wheel. "Yeah, yeah," she said.

I shot a look back to Tak. "You good to go, buddy?"

Tak didn't say anything, his head was still bobbing up and down. I noticed this time his lips were moving. I raised my voice a little. "Tak, you all right, buddy?"

His head jolted, boom, and his eyes laser locked on mine. The way Tak flipped his head toward me almost tossed me right back on my can. June glanced up into the rearview to see why I jerked and why Tak wasn't answering. She snapped him back, all business. "Hey, let's go," she said.

A microsecond, then Tak was back, wham, his whole deal clicked and he recognized me all of a sudden. "Yeah," he said, "Yeah, let's go."

June spun her head over to me, her eyes were wide, I could tell she wanted to be done with that ride. I gave her a quick nod and then pulled myself back three strides and swung my right arm high, toward the med hut.

I yelled, "Clear, clear, clear!"

THREE

Gaz had stayed on alert up in the tower after everyone else was clear, part of standard protocol. Agroland's primary surveillance came from a camera array that fed into the radio room and then streamed to one of the two flat panels in the corner of the cafeteria. The other panel was switched to twenty-four hour Al Jazeera, unless of course there was a football match. I was in the cafeteria having some cardamom-spiced coffee and dates with Tyren and Farid when Max cut Gaz loose. Tyren was another geologist. I thought he was a Brit for the longest time, and then found out he was South

African. Farid was one of the Saudis that had come up to Jordan to 'green the desert.' This was their show really, the Saudis, and they were happy to let everyone know it. There was an aerial plat map wallpapering the cafeteria, a satellite image that showed the northern Arabian Desert and other agro outfits. Giant green circles —crop buttons, Farid called them— peppered the whole bottom of the map, and they had sent a few of their own to show the Jordanians how the deal was done, to pull water from deep down, that type of thing.

Gaz entering the cafeteria meant that Max had cleared his own mind of any threat.

Everyone was pretending a break in routine was a good thing. I could smell the tension. Tak and June were sitting at a table in the corner overlooking the Agrofield. We all pretended not to notice that they weren't touching their trays or making eye contact with each other.

Gaz took a seat with us. He was an electric guy, always cheering everybody up, and we needed some levity. He slid both his hands flat on the table and leaned in like he had a secret to share. That's how Gaz was. He made everyone feel like he was including them in on something special. Farid poured Gaz a coffee. Gaz's eyes shot between the three of us and then he began. "I just spoke with Lucas," he said, and then said nothing else. He slowly raised his cup and sniffed the coffee. He took a sip and then curled his lip.

Tyren leaned in, taking Gaz's bait. "And? What did he say?"

Gaz set the coffee cup down, pursed his lips, and twitched his brow. He darted his eyes across us again. What I said about every one pretending? Well, Gaz was the exception. I guess because he, for one, was loving a break in the routine and was milking the moment for all he could. When he knew he had us, he dropped another tidbit. "He is a westerner."

I took the bait that time. "What do you mean, he is a westerner? How do they know?"

Gaz kept going. "Lucas said Max didn't think the guy was a terrorist either."

Whether or not the stranger was a terrorist was in the front of my mind. When Tak and June arrived at the gate and we didn't all go goodbye boom there was some real relief. Still, the nut jobs could always come knocking.

"He is a westerner, though?" I pressed.

"Oh, he is a westerner. Long, straight white hair. That's what Lucas said. Not a terrorist."

"So what's Max think?" I asked. "A smuggler, journalist, aid worker?"

"A geologist?" asked Tyren.

"Hmm," Gaz said to Tyren. "A geologist."

Tyren smiled, believing he had solved the mystery.

"I don't know," said Gaz. "Lucas didn't say. Could be a geologist or scientist of any kind, maybe a journalist, aid worker, maybe a soldier gone AWOL."

Farid's lips tightened. He sighed through his nose, then said, "Okay, okay. So they have no real idea. Have they figured out where is he from?"

"Maybe," said Gaz.

"Tell us," said Farid.

"Lucas says he was wearing one of those vests with tons of pockets, you know, like photographers wear."

"A photographer," said Farid. "What was he photographing up here?"

"They don't know. No camera, no proper papers, all he had on him was an old side arm, no shells, and a couple of business cards."

Farid raised his hands, "And?"

"Lucas says if he is the guy on the cards then he is from Kenya."

Farid sat back in his chair. A deep frown cut into his face. "That could be anybody's business card."

"Could be," said Gaz. He tapped the side of his head. "Except he had multiple. You would only have multiple of your own cards now, wouldn't you? That is deductive reasoning."

Tyren nodded. "That makes sense. Why would you have a

mess of someone else's cards?"

Gaz nodded in agreement.

"Isn't Kenya quite far?" I asked.

"He must have been traveling and became stranded," said Farid. "Left the road up north."

Gaz sighed, then said, "Yeah, Lucas told me that's exactly what Max said, probably heading to one of the UN camps, got lost, then wandered around for days. The guy is a mess."

"How so?" asked Tyren.

"Well, when I ran into Lucas he told me that guy was dried up like an Egyptian mummy. He said the guy reminded him of bodies he saw in the Iraqi desert."

We all sank in our seats. I'd come across desiccated corpses, like dried up pieces of wood scattered across the desert. Scenes I had put far out of my mind. Tyren and Farid had most likely never witnessed anything so messed up. They looked disgusted all the same.

"How long does Doc figure he'll be around?" asked Tyren.

Gaz sipped more coffee. "I don't know," he said. "Lucas said Wizard is supposed to radio for an airlift once the stranger is stable. Doc is still in there with Jenner, pumping him full of fluids. Figure a day or two."

"Is he awake?" I asked. Farid and Tyren were curious, sure, yet, they would never actually have to spend any time with him. Alone. My time for watch would be soon.

Gaz shook his head. He drifted off for a second, and then he said, "He's been out since they brought him in. He was awake." He nodded toward Tak and June. "When they found him, he was awake."

The three of us went stiff. Agroland was safe, basic but comfortable, if austere. The desert was deadly.

Gaz cleared his throat and leaned in again, "Lucas heard June tell Max that when they brought him in he kept repeating the same thing over and over until he passed out."

Tyren leaned back toward Gaz again, and then in a whisper, he asked him, "What was that?"

Gaz peered over at Tak and June. "June said the guy kept

repeating, 'So many, not enough. So many, not enough.'"

FOUR

After hearing what Lucas had told Gaz, my mind spun back to an inspection I did on my first tour. My patrol was sent into an area of bombed out rubble that had been shock and awed at the beginning of the deal. Like everybody else, we were on a never-ending hunt for WMDs. The buildings were massive, warehouses, or maybe factories, hard to tell with most of the roofs and the walls blown away. We stumbled upon them in the far back of the burnt out shell of a building, desiccated corpses stacked against a still standing door. On the other side of the door, a metal shelving unit was still lodged in place.

Like the Pompeii plaster statues, the bodies were frozen in their fight to escape, fingers clawing, faces wretched, climbing over each other, crushing each other to escape the fumes or smoke or whatever had flooded into the room from the flames beyond the door. They didn't look human anymore. The building had collapsed around them, the ceiling, walls, only the door remained with them, a freaky sculpture, wooden, leathered, mummified.

Throughout the afternoon my mind was spinning. The wrinkled forearm in the back of the SUV, thin, wooden, and brown like tanned leather, desiccated the way the corpses had been. I walked my perimeter patrol and then hit my bunk to rest up before night watch. Flat on my bunk, the images became worse.

By nighttime, most everyone else in Agroland was back in the cafeteria. The break in routine, the stranger, no one was turning in early. They were either playing backgammon or locked on a football match Wizard pulled down from the SKY network. I opted out. I couldn't ever remember the difference between Arsenal or Man United, and I was too high strung to play a board game.

Jenner and I were the only two out in the compound. Jenner, another Brit, was the only other woman on the security team apart from June. She was easy going, tall, athletic, not that hard to look at. Five of the scientists including the Doc were women, so they requested a couple on the security team to ease down on the testosterone.

Agroland was a scientific outpost, which made the place western for the most part. There were a few uptight workers, but the Muslims running the show were laid back. Things were what you would expect. There wasn't any open drinking and we had to watch our language, same as any straight job. Except that after hours, there was definitely some undercover action going on. The head of hydroponics, Adama, was some kind of academic celebrity. All of the women in Agroland melted anytime he walked into a room and rumor was, he was tapping both of the Brit gals on the hydroponics team. Back in

Iraq I had heard about Sunnis having vacation wives. Max told me vacation wives were something different and that the Muslims in Agroland were like anybody else, keeping busy. That was Jenner and me, keeping busy. We weren't an item like Tak and June, but we had spent some playtime in the showers and out in the gazebo in the back of the Agrofield.

I was waiting for Jenner outside of the med hut. Not because we were going to hook up. My turn had come to babysit the stranger. I paced in front of the door until the last possible minute. When the time came for me to open the door of the med hut, I did. I consciously kept to the side of the room opposite the two hospital beds. I was relieved. The stranger was hidden behind a privacy curtain. He'd already had enough exposure to the sun. In the corner, as far as she could be from the bed, was Jenner. She raised her green eyes slowly, silently sighed, and then with a hand on each arm of the chair, raised herself. She gently lifted her weapon, hoisted the strap over her shoulder, and then walked over. She flashed her eyes toward the yard, a gesture for me to follow.

Out in the open, clear of the door, she spun back to me. She shirked her shoulders high. I heard a shudder escape her lips and imagined a tremor in her spine. Her spine must have quivered, because she pulled her shoulders back and arched her waist outward to counter whatever she was feeling. Her stretch thrusted her breasts toward me. She was not wearing her sports bra and those pert nipples punctuating that cotton tank top should have switched on a few familiar gears. The sinking look in her eyes killed any of those type of thoughts.

Jenner had that same distant intensity that June had at the gate.

She pressed her lips together and then absently peered over my shoulder, out past the fence. I hadn't heard anything. I don't think she heard a sound out there either. She turned her head back to me, closed her eyes tight, opened them, and then squeezed her eyes tight and opened them a second time. I recognized what she was doing, self-calming. "That guy creeps me out," she finally said. Jenner's Brit accent was very proper except, unlike Gareth, the tone didn't make her pompous. She raised her hands to warm her bare arms. I said nothing. I should have because Jenner tilted her head and hit me with a leer that said she wasn't a nut.

"Yeah," I said, catching on. "I'm creeped out too, and I haven't even been in there yet."

She nodded and scrunched her face in agreement. She rubbed her arms a bit harder, and then began to turn back and forth toward the fence in an attempt to keep warm. "I know it's not that cold," she said, and then she gave me a schoolgirl grin, "but I kind of got the chills."

I returned her smile and then said, "No, I think it's cooling off at night now, fall and all. You remember, hot all day then," I shook my head side to side. "Sorry, I'd offer you my shirt."

"Don't be silly," she said. She was quick to recoup, a soldier after all. "I'll head to the caf. I know where there's a stash of hot cocoa mix."

"There you go," I said. "They're all in there. Expect Tak and June."

Jenner's eyes widened. "Gazebo?"

I gave her a shy nod. "Gazebo." The gazebo across the Agrofield was the only private place in Agroland.

"Well, I don't blame them," she said, nodding her head. "A distraction could be due right about now." She shot me a smile. "Anyway, I wanted to touch base before…"

I cut her off. "Yeah," I said. "I get it."

Jenner began to step backward toward the cafeteria. "Okay, maybe I'll see you after your shift then."

I gave her a wave. "You bet," I said, and then she was gone and I was alone in front of the med hut.

I dropped the M16 from my shoulder, left the door open, and went directly to the corner of the room where I had found Jenner. I spun and planted myself down with my weapon across my lap, no differently than a thousand times on duty, no differently than when I was a kid hunting back home.

I fixed my eyes on the two feet of floor between me and the end of the bed. The odor of the ointments Doc had rubbed on the stranger made me want to puke. I could remember the smell of salves when I had stuck my head into the med hut the first time, but in the corner, up close to the bed, the stench was overwhelming, a twisted mix of antiseptic and baby's ass.

I began to breathe through my mouth. My eyes followed the floor toward the open door. I sucked my chest full and then relaxed and tried to focus on the outside.

That was a mistake.

Between the bed and privacy curtain was a small dim lamp. Enough light for my peripheral to catch the forearm on the side of the bed, a dark shadow against the cream white of the sheet. The same thin forearm from that had been flashing through my mind since the stranger arrived.

I couldn't help myself but to look again.

Doc had fastened an IV drip to the stranger. I could not imagine how she had found a vein in that thin rail of an arm.

The side of my neck tightened to force my eyes back toward the door. Instead, my eyes shifted up to the dark, naked shoulder. Ointments and low light lessened the leathered wooden texture, yet the thinness of the emaciated shoulder could not be hidden, darkened skin taut against sinew and bone. I am not sure how long I locked onto the shoulder. Time slipped. At some point, as if the limb released them, my eyes moved across the flattened chest up to the wick of a neck, and the gaunt skeletal head of the desert survivor. Draped long to the sides of his face, fine white hair that glowed brighter than his pillowcase, blonde hair bleached from the sun. His narrow jaw jutted from what at one time must have been a strong profile and his cheeks sucked in high toward the hollow sockets of his eyes. His eyes were captivating crystal blue pools, lucid, clear, pure, shocking large white orbs that peered out over the bed and into my own. I stared at the man for quite some time. Not until he spoke did my brain kick in. The stranger was peering at me. He was awake, and from the bloody remnants of his lips, a cadence flowed.

"So many, not enough. So many, not enough."

FIVE

The med hut became a full house. I'm not sure why I dozed, must've been the fumes from the ointments and salves slathered all over the stranger. He had woken while I was on watch and I'd sat there staring at him for I don't know how long. When I realized what was happening, I hopped on the two-way and bam, I had the full brigade.

Doc, Max, Gareth, and Alfie were in the med hut with me and the rest of the camp was outside the door. Alfie was the Jordanian scientist in charge. His real name was something complicated so everyone called him Alfie. He was older than everyone else in Agroland, always smiling, not at all condescending like Gareth. Gareth bullied his way in to represent the Brit contingency, I guess. Max was security of course, Doc was the Doc, and me, I was still on watch.

Max, Alfie, Gareth, and I were huddled at the foot of the bed. I was confined between them and the wall. We were all uncomfortable. Not one of us wanted to be in the presence of this abnormally ill man.

We watched Doc do her thing at the stranger's bedside. She flashed a penlight above his eyes and in an elevated voice she asked him, "Are you okay, sir? Can you hear me?" He kept on peering forward and in the same soft raspy rhythm, kept repeating the same phrase. "So many, not enough. So many, not enough."

Gareth was the first to say something, "How long has he been saying that? That phrase?"

"Since he woke up," I said. "He sounds British, like Tak and June said."

"The dialect," said Gareth.

"East African," said Max. "I'd say Tanzanian or Kenyan."

Alfie adjusted his wire-rimmed glasses and held up the small browned card that had been found in the stranger's pocket. "That's what this card says. Shame he has no other papers. They must have been lost. I'm surprised he was still dressed at all."

"Has to be the only reason he's alive," said Doc. "You each had the training. He was wearing full pants, a vest, and a long sleeve button down. Without those, he would have died hours sooner in the heat of the summer," she went on to say, "you can lose nineteen liters of water a day out there, a quarter your body weight. This time of year, five liters a day. The clothes slowed the dehydration."

Max tightened his jaw. "Thank you, Doctor. So by that measure, how many days was he out there?"

"By his size, a healthy male, two meters height," Doc pressed her lower lip up then added, "And we are near autumn. More than most I figure, four, five days max."

"Five days," I said. I had been desert trained in the military, again, when I signed up for Agroland. I had been told what could happen with exposure.

Max shook his head. "His brains must be pan fried."

Alfie read the card aloud, "Justin Caruthers, Professional Hunter & Photographer, safari & guide services, and there is an address in Nairobi, Kenya."

The stranger stopped chanting. Alfie peered over the rim of his glasses toward the man. "Justin Caruthers, is that you, sir?"

The stranger stopped his chant. His large eyes rolled in their socket to meet Alfie's. Alfie cleared his throat. "Hrum, Mister Caruthers, you are quite safe. You were found, or shall I say rescued, in the desert. We will arrange for transportation to a medical facility."

Still the stranger was silent.

Max raised a brow toward Doc. "Is he coherent?"

Alfie raised his voice an octave higher. "Do you understand, Mister Caruthers?"

This time the survivor responded, his gravelly speech dragged, unsure of the word, "Caruthers."

"Yes," said Alfie. "The card we found on your person reads Justin Caruthers. Are you Justin Caruthers?"

As he scanned our faces, the stranger's orbs appeared to swell and float into and then out of his sockets. "Yes," he said, and then paused, struggling to gain control of his mouth. "Justin Caruthers, that is my name."

The stranger spoke naturally, raspy, without the cadence of the mantra. And yet there was nothing natural in his appearance. To watch him speak in his emaciated condition was ghastly. What had been hidden in shadow was exaggerated by light. His jaw was too gaunt and moved mechanically. His flesh was desiccated, ruined. Ulcerated blisters and sores seethed beneath the slather of ointment. He was not openly bleeding, yet with each twitch and word the blood threatened to surface from behind the taut veil of skin that once had been a face. While mindlessly wording his mantra, the stranger's mouth had barely opened. To form the new words, he had to force what was left of his crepe paper lips up and away from his teeth. Teeth that, like his hair and eyes, were unnaturally white and appeared too long for his dried up head.

Gaz and Wizard were in the doorframe of the med hut and relayed word back to the others close behind that the survivor had spoken. They craned their necks toward the curtain divider shielding their view of the bed.

Doc placed her stethoscope against the survivor's frail chest and began to speak to her patient. Her authoritarian Cambridge accent shifted in tone to soft and maternal. Her reassuring bedside manner was soothing even to me. "Welcome, Mister Caruthers," she said. "Do you know where you are?"

"No," he said.

"You are at a scientific research facility. You were found in the desert and brought here."

"Yes," he said. "Yes, I remember, I was in the desert. For quite some time."

"I imagine you were. Can you follow this light, please?" Doc clicked her pen light back on and waved the beam left to right above Caruthers' eyes.

"I wandered and then there was a truck," he said. "And two people."

"That's right, Mister Caruthers, two people brought you here," she said. "You are in very serious condition. We will have you airlifted out once you are stable."

"I see," said Caruthers.

Gareth stepped slightly closer to the bed. "Mister Caruthers?"

Caruthers' eyes darted past Doc to the foot of the bed.

"Yes," said Caruthers, appearing coherent.

Gareth jumped right in. "My name is Gareth," he said. "We need to ask you a couple of questions."

"I understand," said Caruthers.

The corners of Gareth's mouth slipped up, a faint smile. He asked him straight out, "Do you remember how you ended up in the desert?"

And Caruthers answered. He answered all right. "Yes, I believe so," he said. "Yes, yes I do. I will tell you. First, could I please have some water?"

SIX

Whatever trance Justin Caruthers had been in had lifted. Doc held the bottle of water he had requested in front of him, a bendy straw from the cafeteria bobbing out of the top. Caruthers' mouth was so worn he was barely able to secure a hold on the straw, his long lizard-like tongue darted out around the end, rapidly lapping any fluid he managed to suck through. The whole while he drank his huge orbs continued to float from Max, to Gareth, to Alfie, then me, and then back again to Max. When Doc pulled the water away from him, the bottle still looked full.

"Not enough," he said.

"I will give you more in a moment," said Doc. "Too much will shock you. Your fluids should come from the IV."

Caruthers glanced at his forearm. "Yes, the IV."

Caruthers was beginning to appear to me as someone trapped in a costume. A ghoulish disguise that reeked so bad our eyes watered and our stomachs turned.

Gareth pressed him. "I am sure these inconveniences will pass in due time," he said. "Now, if you could be so kind as to share with us how you came to find yourself alone in the desert."

Caruthers nodded. "I understand. You gentlemen are running a tight camp. You need to know the lay of the land." He stopped talking to let a faint gurgle escape from the back of his throat, and then continued, "So to speak."

Doc scrunched her face. "This cannot take long."

Caruthers' head pivoted toward her. "Everything is quite all right, Doctor," he said. "I need to share this story." I half expected his head to wobble off his pencil thin neck when he swung back to us. In some way, he did appear to be all right, stronger anyway. Even from the small amount of water, Caruthers was revitalized.

"Gareth, yes?" he said.

Gareth nodded. "Yes."

Caruthers began his story. His words came slow and unrushed, his voice silken from his dried gravel throat.

"I did not go out alone," he began. "My partner, Sven Lambert, and I led a group of anthropologists and documentarians to the remote Omo Valley."

"The Omo Valley?" asked Gareth. "In Ethiopia?"

"North of Lake Turkana," said Caruthers. "To study the Hamar tribe. We were there for four weeks without issue. When the time came to leave, we planned to travel southeast toward Nairobi, the way we had come in. The second night out was when they came."

"When they came?" asked Gareth.

"Yes," said Caruthers. Again, his blue eyes swelled forward

and back into his sockets. "So many of them, from the darkness. They were heavily painted, screaming scarified nightmares."

"A war clan," said Max.

Caruthers was quiet for a few seconds and then said, "Exactly, a warring clan. Perhaps they thought we were with the Hamar tribe we had been visiting. Perhaps they were angry because we were trespassing. We would never find out. The attack was swift and fatal. Sven, I, and the few others that could began an immediate futile fight in the darkness. We were overtaken."

Caruthers made a long dry sucking sound that made the back of my neck quiver.

His head again pivoted slowly toward Doc. "Could you please be so kind?"

She placed the straw to his wounded mouth again, and again his lizard tongue leapt out to pull in the water he needed to rinse his throat. After a long moment, Doc moved the water bottle away from him.

"Where was I?" he asked.

Keen to the story, Max had moved his hands onto his hips. His elbows bowed outward. The idea of a war clan had drawn his attention. "You were overtaken," he said.

"Yes, that is right," said Caruthers. "We were overwhelmed."

"How many were you?" asked Max.

"The anthropologists, the film crew, the porters, eighteen people, plus Sven and myself."

"So many," said Gareth.

"Not enough," Caruthers snapped.

"Not enough," repeated Alfie.

The icicle blue of Caruthers' eyes beamed intensely and his orbs appeared to grow as they pushed forward. "In their fury," he said. "They ransacked our camp. What they did not want to keep, they used to fuel a bonfire, and then they threw our dead into the flames and began to dance around the blaze."

"They burnt them?" asked Gareth.

"They cooked them."

Gareth winced. "What do you mean they cooked them?"

"Cooked them," said Caruthers. "They feasted on eight of us while those that survived, bound by our hands and feet, watched, screaming, begging for the savages to yield."

Alfie jerked his glasses from his face, pulled a cloth from his pocket, and hurriedly began to wipe the lenses. "Excuse me," he said. "Did you say they feasted on your party?"

"One of the anthropologists had a word for them," said Caruthers. "She called them Anthropophagi."

Almost under his breath, Gareth recited a strange verse I will never forget. "Then come the tribes of Africa," he said. "West of the Ethiopian kingdom; the Agriophagi, the Wild-beast-eaters, who live chiefly on the flesh of panthers and lions; the Pamphagi, the Eat-alls, who devour everything; and the Anthropophagi, the Man-eaters, whose diet is human flesh."

"That is correct," said Caruthers. "The Man-eaters."

"They don't exist," said Gareth. "The tribes are myth from ancient Greek, like the Cynocephali."

"Cynocephali?" I asked.

Gareth raised a brow to me in that condescending way he does to everybody. "The dog headed tribes of India, recorded in the Natural History written by Pliny the Elder in 77 AD. These tribes are ancient folklore." Then to enunciate the obvious he said thickly, "As I said, they don't exist."

"I assure you, Gareth," said Caruthers, the words raspy and full of breath. "The Man-eaters, regardless of name, are quite real, as the young anthropologist would find out. Her and the other two women in our party had it the worst."

"They raped them?" asked Alfie.

"No, not at all," Caruthers went on. "The next day they hung her from a pole, and while she was still alive, sliced off pieces of her well-endowed breasts. The other two women soon shared her fate."

Alfie's complexion paled. "Alive?" he asked. "They were butchered alive?"

"Yes," said Caruthers. "Alive." His reply was matter of fact. "That is exactly what they did. They kept her and the other two women alive. Eating them slowly while the others, the men, were spared the prolonged torture. The men were skinned alive, one by one. Skinned, the men died so much quicker."

Alfie grimaced again, keeping his eyes tight as he slipped his glasses back over the bridge of his nose. He peered at Caruthers, sucked in a breath, and then asked what we all wanted to know. "And you? You escaped?"

Caruthers' reply was rapid, "I alone escaped."

"And all of the others?" asked Alfie.

"Eaten," said Caruthers. "They were all feasted upon."

Max interrupted. "Do you know where you are?"

"North," said Caruthers, attentive to the question. "Far north."

Alfie cleared his throat again, "Hrum. You are ten thousand kilometers from where this tribe attacked you."

Caruthers said nothing. When he had spoken a moment before, his humanity made him appear a victim. A victim trapped in a wounded body. Silent, that humanity had left him. He had transformed into something not human at all. The sheets of blisters covering his burnt skin were shiny from the medicated ointments, his white hair was no different than tight strands of spider silk, and his blue eyes were too clear, too wide, too bulbous. Silent, Caruthers was a cadaver.

Only when he spoke again did his humanity return.

His tone changed. His confidence was gone, replaced by a saddened confusion, almost a regret. "Ten thousand kilometers," he said. "I had no way of knowing." He paused again and I thought we had lost him, and then he continued, apologetic in the way he described what happened. "They pursued me relentlessly," he said. "I found shelter, safety with others, each time they arrived in the night. I escaped through the hills, the desert, safety again and then, again they came."

"And those providing you safety?" asked Gareth skeptically.

Caruthers was jarred in his reply. "Killed, murdered, feasted upon, I'm sure."

Max was next. "How long since the last attack?"

Caruthers was beginning to drift. "I am not sure," he said. "A long time. I kept moving north, away from them."

Max nodded his head. "I am sure you did."

"You cannot imagine," said Caruthers. "So many, not enough. So many, not enough." He paused again and then fell back into his cadence. "So many, not enough. So many, not enough."

SEVEN

After Caruthers slipped back into his trance, Max, Gareth, and Alfie wasted no time leaving the med hut. Gaz and Wizard were blankly staring back from the door. In the shadows around them, the others huddled close. They were spared seeing Caruthers, but they'd heard every twisted word he had said. I opened my eyes wide at Gaz and shrugged my shoulders. He shook his head back at me and then disappeared with the others.

That left Doc and me in the med hut. Her authoritarian Cambridge was back. "You're going to need to keep a close eye on him," she said. "Despite his improved condition, I will need to give him a sedative."

She stuck a needle into the base of the IV drip. A faint cloud spun into the solution and then dissipated. She wiggled the drip bag from the bottom and said, "This one is very mild yet should have the desired outcome. If he begins to convulse, send for me."

"Convulse. You aren't going to stay?" I asked.

Doc's lips tightened back and shrugged into her cheeks in a 'Don't know what to tell you' fashion.

"Listen," she said. "You will know in the next twenty minutes if he's going to have a negative reaction to the sedative. After that, he will be out for hours." She smiled. "You can get some shut eye."

"I don't think Max would see things that way," I said.

She gave me the same shrugged look and with a hint of intolerance added, "Suit yourself." And that was the end of that.

The solution must've been doing something though. Caruthers' creepy cadence had already slowed to a purr and his bright eyes were dropping to a close.

Doc had her back to Caruthers and me as she sorted her med kit. "See," she said. I guess her experience and the sound of his voice were enough to tell her what was happening.

"I'll be fine," I told her. "I'll let you know if anything happens."

Finished with her side tray, she dimmed the lamp again and then made her way to the door. When I turned my head back to Caruthers, he was already asleep. Whatever she'd stuck in his IV had knocked him out.

In the dim light, Caruthers was tolerable. His dark skin was no less blistered and oily, and his was frame still far too skeletal to be real, but he was nowhere near as shocking as he had appeared under full light, awake and talking.

When the time came for me to turn over my watch, I stepped outside the med hut and keyed my two-way. "Wizard, where are you?" The two-way stayed silent. I keyed the radio again. "Wizard, c'mon," I said. "Get over here." Wizard was up for sure. Prime time was about to hit the states and he lived to download all of his shows. I was about to key again when he came back over the two-way. "I'm here," he said.

"Get over here," I said.

He keyed back, "Is that guy knocked out?"

"Doesn't matter," I said. "C'mon."

"All right, give me a minute." Maybe in some fantasy, he was expecting me to beg for a double watch.

I heard the side door of the Greenhouse slam shut. His rifle was slung over his back and both of his hands were cupped around his front, fixing his fly.

"C'mon," I said, coaching him forward.

"Sorry," he said. "I had work to do."

"Yeah. I bet."

When he was closer, he asked, "What do you think about what that guy said?"

"Sounded crazy," I said. "I never heard anything quite like that."

"Me either." He paused then he added, "The dwarves think he's a jinn."

On our first day in Agroland, Jenner had nicknamed a group of the Jordanian workers after some of the dwarves in Snow White —Happy, Sleepy, Grumpy, Bashful, and Dopey —because we didn't know any of their names. The names stuck and they fit because the dwarves were the ones that did all of the real grunt work. They didn't appear to mind, though I don't think anybody called them those names to their faces. Their English wasn't that good and they kept to themselves. Wizard was the only one on the security team fluent in Arabic, so he was the only one that talked to them.

"I'll bite," I said. "What's a Jinn?"

"You know," he grinned. "A genie."

"You mean like three wishes?" I snickered and scratched the back of my head. "I guarantee you they got that wrong."

"Not the Hollywood kind of genie. To the Muslims, Satan is a Jinn. They think Caruthers is demon or a dragon, assuming human form to mislead and destroy his human victims. They were already whispering some anti-Jinn prayer."

"A demon?" I asked.

"Oh yeah," he said. "Jinn can be good or evil. They can change form, have the power to travel great distances at extreme speeds, and are full of magic."

"Magic," I said. "They told you that?"

"No, of course not," he said. "I saw that on some sci-fi show."

He had never been in the field, had never seen anything other than special effects from the shows he downloaded.

"I gotta go," I said.

He gave me one of his tough little kid looks. "Are you gonna be up?"

"Yeah," I nodded and turned out to the yard. "For a bit. I need a shower. If you need anything, ping me."

He returned the nod. "Yeah, okay."

"Did you get a look at him when the SUV came in?"

"No," he said. "I was looking underneath the truck."

"Hmm."

"Why?" he asked.

"Well, you had the best of it," I told him. "Take my advice. Keep your head down until morning and you'll do yourself a favor."

Wizard nodded again. "Right."

I spun toward the head, relieved to be out of there. I forgot to ask Wizard what time he had radioed in for Caruthers' pickup. Anytime soon would be good. There were only eight of us and Max wasn't going to pull a watch, so my turn to sit with the dried up husk would come around again soon.

I showered up and then headed back to the med hut. This was Wizard's first time with the stranger so I figured I would check on him before hooking up with Jenner.

The door to the med hut was still open. I poked my head in, winced, and jerked back. Having rinsed my sinuses in the shower, the reek of the med hut hit me in a new perverse way.

I sucked a deep breath in through my mouth and then peered in again.

The chair in the corner was empty.

My muscles tightened up through the back of my neck. I couldn't believe that Wizard bagged on his post.

"Psst," I said. "Wiz, are you in there?"

There was no answer.

I didn't want to see Caruthers again, but I needed to be sure that Wizard wasn't passed out next to the bed. I headed toward the curtain and prepared to peek around the side. Maybe Caruthers had died. Perhaps Wizard had booked it out of the med hut to get Doc. I sucked another breath through my mouth and then stuck my head around the corner.

The bed was empty.

To the side of the bed, nothing, only the IV drip dangling from the suspended bag. I grabbed the foot of the bed and propelled myself to the other side. There on the floor, sticking out from under the hospital bed, was the stock of a rifle. I dropped to the side of the bed. Alone on the floor was Wizard's M16.

With a jolt, I was upright. The room blurred as I spun toward the door. I keyed my two-way. "Wizard, I'm in the med hut. Where are you?"

That was when I heard the muffled boom.

EIGHT

I booked it out into the yard without bothering to key the two-way again. I wanted to identify where the explosion had come from. The fence lights began to flicker and then went out. I full stopped. All of the lights were out, the Greenhouse, the pods, the utility buildings. Above and around me the small flood lamps that were attached to each of the surveillance camera battery packs came to life in a cascade of sharp clicks, dotting the compound with tight little cones of light. The mini-flood lamps contrasted against the night, leaving darkened voids in the spaces in between.

I was in one of the darkened voids.

Apart from the tight circles lit by the cones, I was blind. My hands were barely visible in front of me.

The door of the security barracks opened and I caught a brief glimpse of Max as he marched through the light cast by the little flood mounted above. On the edge of the flood, Max was a hard lined silhouette, standing tall, chest up, elbows out, and fists at his waists. Gaz and Lucas came next and flanked him beneath the flood. Max raised his left arm to his head to speak to the rest of the security team on his headset. I switched to the alert channel. Max raised his other arm, the distinct outline of his MP5 jutting out to his side. He waved high right and then high left. Gaz and Lucas each bolted into one of those directions. Then Max walked directly toward me, backlit by the barracks light.

As he closed in, I readied to identify myself. His voice came before his face. "Something must have overloaded the power," he said. "I want you to head over to the pods with Lucas and Jenner instead of the gate, and ready your weapon, Aker. I want us to look good." I flipped my head back behind me and realized I was between Max and the tower flood. Max was not blind at all. My silhouette gave me away.

That's when the scream came.

A single curdle of surprise, cut short. By the timbre, a younger man's voice, one of the Jordanian dwarves. Max dropped his inflection to a whisper. "Bloody hell. That came from behind the Greenhouse."

I flung my M16 from my shoulder and jerked the bolt. "Yeah," I said. "Definitely from behind the Greenhouse."

"Gaz is already over there," he said. "That's where the explosion came from. Get with Lucas and Jenner, round everyone up, and I'll go have a look-see."

From inside the med hut, I could not tell if the muffled boom had come from the Powerhouse or the Greenhouse. Max had a better bearing from the barracks. Behind the Greenhouse made sense. A series of pumps and the central air units were in the back of the Greenhouse, right under the electrical panels that ran to the lights. They would be more likely to affect the lights if they blew than any one of the ton batteries in the Powerhouse. Apart from two small natural gas backup generators, all the Powerhouse held was the batteries. That and the leads to the compounds underground gas and electric.

"Is that where Wizard is?" I asked.

"No," said Max. "He's on watch in the med hut."

"He's not," I said, "and neither is Caruthers."

"What do you mean?" Max was becoming less pleased by the second.

"I mean the med hut is empty," I said. "I went to check on him and then heard the blast."

Max shook his head. "Bloody hell," he said again. "I didn't think that creepy crispy could even move. You have your torch?"

I threw a hand down onto my gear belt. "Yeah."

Max started toward the Greenhouse. "Plug it in and go," he said. "I'll see you inside."

"Right," I said. Max had already disappeared into the darkness. He wasn't bothering with a light.

I had mixed emotions about fixing a light to my weapon, though I wasn't about to question Max. I snapped the hi-def light into the mount on the end of my M16 muzzle and headed toward the other floating orbs already gathering over by the pods.

My heart thumped hard in my chest. The bright eleven hundred lumens LED mounted on the end of my M16 was a floating beacon and I was wearing nothing more than cargo pants and a light cotton button up. If a shot came out of the darkness, I had no protection, no cover on my head, no jacket, I would shred. If I heard a shot, I would kill the light. The job to focus on was to get everyone to a single location.

The pods didn't have separate cameras on each so there was no line of light cones above the doorways. The few light poles that stood amidst the dwellings only lit up small circles directly below.

I headed directly toward Lucas. The bright LED on the end of his weapon cut far up into the darkness like a sabre. The swarm of headlamps to his side bobbed in little circles like large fireflies.

I winced as three of the scientists faced me at the same time, not realizing they were blinding me.

"Hey. Look away, will ya?"

"Adjust your lenses, please, gentlemen, ladies," said Gareth, his tone as condescending as ever.

"Aker," Gareth continued, "Your colleague here has not enlightened us as to what is going on. Please do tell what brings us out here."

"You know the drill," I said. "A trip to the Greenhouse."

The effort to even speak to the security team must've irked him. With a grumble, he asked, "And why do we need to do that?"

"As you can see," I said kindly. "The lights are out."

I was not about to tell Gareth any more than he needed to know.

Gareth persisted, "We heard a scream."

Jenner's voice cut the darkness, "Someone was probably hurt when the lights blew."

Another swarm of fireflies closed in from around the corner. With no light of her own, Jenner had gathered the dwarves from their barracks. Where the scientists had been quick to pour into the yard, the workers had most likely chosen to sit tight.

As he always did, Gareth eased up for Jenner. "You believe someone was hurt?" he asked. "Is there anything we can do?"

"Thank you, Doctor," she said in a singsong reply. "Once we are in the Greenhouse, I believe you can help to sort this all out."

Alfie chimed in, "Is anyone unaccounted for?"

A headlamp flooded Jenner's torso, then face. She shielded her eyes with her M16. "Please," she said.

"Sorry," said Alfie.

"Two men were unaccounted for in the barracks," she said.

"The other seven are here with me."

From one of the bobbing headlamps near me came another female voice, Hannah, a Brit hydroponics expert. "Bobo and Asef are in the Greenhouse," she said. "They are running pressure checks through the night."

"Those are the two," said Jenner.

The scream had come from either Bobo or Asef, the two Jordanian drillers that doubled as plumbers for the hydroponics team. The math was easy for everyone else to figure as well.

Another lady Brit spoke, the other hydroponics engineer, Carver, "We best get inside. One of the pumps must have blown."

"That blast did not sound like a pump to me," said Gareth.

"Easily a pump," said Hakim, the Saudi drill engineer and last word on the matter. Gareth's face was hidden in the darkness, but I'm sure he swallowed some comeback.

Lucas' sabre spun above the group. "Gentleman, ladies," he began. "Let's do as we practiced and everything will be dealt with. I count twelve, everyone present from the pods. Mister Aker and Miss Jenner will lead the way to the Greenhouse, followed by the party from the pods, then the party from the barracks, and I will be in the rear as we have rehearsed."

Jenner playfully bumped my side with her hip, then slipped in front of me for the short walk across the compound. From the sounds of the discussion, the whole deal was a mechanical mishap, no reason to be alarmed. Apart from Gareth's expected grumbling, I didn't hear any complaints. Taft and Hakim would set to work on fixing the issue, Doc would take care of wounded Bobo, or Asef, whichever one of them that had gotten hurt, and in minutes, the lights would be back on.

What no one was aware of was that Caruthers and Wizard were missing.

Nothing new had come over the security channel in the moments since I left Max.

We were all walking in the dark.

NINE

The dull blue hue of the large LED panel filled the cafeteria. The corners of the room flickered as quadrants of the screen flashed from one camera to another. The same glow that would have been cozy on a sports night felt eerie. Jenner and I flanked the cafeteria door as everyone filed in from the hallway and planted themselves at the tables. Good lemmings ultimately doing what they were told. Except, of course, for Gareth. He followed Alfie, Hakim, and Taft across the cafeteria to the edge of the Greenhouse proper where, arms crossed, Max awaited their arrival.

Tyren was fidgeting with the remote control for the sat box Wizard had mounted between the panels. "I don't suppose the dish will turn on?" he asked.

"Sorry, mate," said Gaz. He was across the room next to Max. "The panel is tied into separate battery packs."

Tyren raised his hands in frustration. "What does that mean?" he asked.

Farid was sitting next to his friend. "The cameras, motion sensors, and display tie into a backup, the sat box is on the main."

Tyren flashed a glance to Gaz. Gaz shrugged in agreement. Tyren grimaced. "Well, where's Wizard?" he asked. "Maybe he can put something on for us while we wait."

"Wizard is checking the tower," said Max, his attention sudden and focused.

I leered at Max. He had no idea where Wizard was.

Lucas entered the cafeteria, the last of the outside party. Even though I usually would be at the gate with Wizard, I was well aware how this went down. Jenner waited by the entrance until everyone filed in, and then they did another headcount.

Under her breath, Jenner slipped out, "Bloody hell."

My eyes darted to Jenner, her lips moving as she counted, and then out to the tables to count myself. Gareth, Alfie, Hakim, and Taft were over with Max and Gaz. Farid and Tyren were at the table next to me with both of the female botanists, the Brit Sam and the Jordanian Maryam. Behind them at the table near the window were Doc, Adama, Hannah, and the other female member of the hydroponics team, Carver, altogether an even dozen. The cooks, Adnan and Ahmed, sat at one of the two back tables and the dwarves at the other. Between the cooks and the dwarves, there should have been seven, except there weren't. I scanned the room again. Dopey and Bashful were not at any of the tables.

"Bloody hell is right," said Lucas. The phrase sounded peculiar coming from him. Lucas was a Native American Indian, except Canadian, or Canadian Indian, I didn't know the right term. He told me he was a member of the Odawa and I was quite all right with that. People have the wrong idea about Canadians thinking they are always passive. They fight and die like everybody else. Soldiers are soldiers.

"Are you sure you weren't off?" asked Lucas.

"I'm sure," said Jenner. "Dopey was the first out the door."

"Well, you're two short," he said.

I turned away from the tables and spoke in a low voice so only Jenner and Lucas could hear me. "This is bad."

Jenner and Lucas locked eyes on me.

"What do you know, Aker?" asked Lucas.

"We need to get over to Max," I said.

Jenner, in the most casual way, slid her hand free from her M16 up to my top button, slipped her fingers inside, and then tugged. Flirtatious yet serious, she asked, "What's going on?"

I tightened my jaw. I was embarrassed I hadn't told them earlier and at the same time guilty for not waiting for Max. "Caruthers," I said.

Jenner wrinkled her nose, "What about him?"

"I'm not hauling that freak in here," said Lucas.

"No," I said. "You don't have to. He's up and moving around."

"Who was watching him?" asked Jenner. "Wizard, right?"

I hesitated to say anything.

"Out with it," she said.

Unsure of what to say and not wanting the slightest chance of being heard by anyone else, I mumbled, "Wizard's sort of missing."

Lucas peered toward Gaz and Max. "Max said Wizard was checking the tower, but there is no way he would have ordered Wizard out of the med hut. That means he has no idea where Wizard is."

Lucas was on the ball. Even I missed that slip. Jenner said what I was thinking, "Won't be too long before the brains in the room catch on." She released my shirt.

The timing was right because that was when Max called us over from across the room, "Lucas, Jenner, Aker." I spun around toward Max, his hand beckoning us with closed fingers in the Arab fashion.

From the back of my ear, I heard Jenner say in a low whisper, "And the hits just keep on coming."

TEN

Whatever the leadership team was talking about stopped when we walked up. Max must have clued them in because not one of them had the same light look on their face they had come in with. Hakim and Taft seamed concerned and Alfie looked sick. Gareth, for a change, was upbeat. He had a stillness about him that separated him from the group. His eyes peered past Max, the wheels spinning up there in that uptight head.

Max started right in, "Jenner, you stay in here and keep the calm. Lucas, Aker, you two head out with Taft and Hakim to see about getting the lights back. Gaz and I are going to see if we can round up Tak and June. They aren't answering their channel." He scowled. "And then we're going to go about finding Wizard and our missing friend."

"Max," said Jenner, her voice hesitant.

"Yeah," he said.

Jenner raised her chin. "We have another problem."

"Let's add one to the list," said Max. "C'mon, spit."

"We're missing two of the workers," said Jenner.

Alfie dropped his jaw and Gareth returned from wherever his brain had taken him.

Max's forehead wrinkled, "Why didn't you radio in from outside?"

"That's part of the problem." Jenner's eyes went wide. "They left the barracks with me and they're not here now."

Max leered at Lucas. He'd created the protocols so he was well aware that Lucas was to tail the group. "What happened? They pass you going to the head?"

Lucas shrugged one corner of his mouth, "Everyone filed in fine. If she says they were there, then they ghosted."

"Or were ghosted," added Gaz.

Alfie sucked a large breath through his teeth and then asked, "Which two? Do you know?" With a furrowed brow, he began to scan the faces at the tables, triggering those sitting to begin doing the same.

Jenner didn't answer immediately. She first tightened and then bit into her lips.

Max prodded her, "Well, which two?"

"Dopey and Bashful," said Jenner. She dropped her head slightly after she spoke to avoid the scolding glare she knew was coming.

"Excuse me," said Alfie, still scanning the tables. "Dopey and Bashful? I don't understand."

Gareth interceded, "Saeed and Wal. The teams have taken to giving affectionate nicknames to each other. Like your name, Alfie."

Alfie pursed his lip and then bobbed his head. "Yes, of

course, Dopey and Bashful. Well, where could they be?"

"We'll find them," said Max.

The side of Gareth's cheek sucked in and up, he was about to exert some authority.

Gareth had more tells than an oncoming train.

He had no authority to directly assert. Every one of the scientists held a fistful of PhDs, and more than half of them held a title that could sway what happened in Agroland. Farid and Hakim were the Saudi consultants with the purse strings backing the project, plus Hakim ran the drill team. Doc had her own set of keys and protocols. Max ran the security team, Adama the hydroponics, and Alfie ran the botanists as well as being the general director of the whole compound. As Agroland's glorified mechanic, even Taft had more title than Gareth.

Gareth swung his influence with pure old school Anglo-Saxon certainty, and something else. Gareth had the personality of a predator. He found weakness and vulnerability an opportunity. Alfie was a bookworm and the other leads at Agroland were so caught up in their own work that they simply didn't care to be involved in power plays.

Gareth was different. Power plays were all he had.

I wasn't sure if anyone other than Max could tell he was sizing up the group for his strike, or maybe they didn't care. Max wasn't going to shut him down, at least not harshly. Gareth could easily have Max dismissed from his position, especially if the evenings events were cross-examined by the company. Gareth did have that influence, but then so did every other scientist. Gareth's tongue rubbed the side of that sucked in cheek. He rubbed his chin with his index and middle finger. His eyes, dark and thoughtful, darted across the faces of his colleagues and then the security team.

So many tells.

Gareth raised his hand from his chin to swath back the length of his sandy brown hair.

A twinkle in his eye and then, as casual as a talk on a walk, "What did Caruthers say, 'they pursued him relentlessly, each time they came in the night?' Maybe he was playing us from the get go. Maybe he had some friends waiting beyond the perimeter."

Max didn't hesitate, "There are motion sensors on the fence."

"True," said Gareth. "Perhaps if one of his friends made their way in, moved Caruthers, and then shut off the power to knock out the motion sensors."

Alfie began to tremble. "Is that what happened? How did they get in? Are there more coming in now?"

Max's stayed calm and kept his voice even, but he could not hide the breath that raised his chest a full fist. "There is no way anyone could have gotten in and moved him."

"What if?" asked Gareth. "What if the motion sensors went down? Are they up right now? How do we know?"

"Yes," said Alfie, putty in Gareth's hands. "How do we know?"

Taft and Hakim glanced at each other and then at Max.

Gareth tilted his head back and in the most matter of fact tone said, "Caruthers told us some spook story to throw us off, and then shut down the power so they could get in."

"That's not possible," said Max.

Gaz, always charged, jumped in, "When they found him, he was delirious. He kept saying how many there had been and not enough to defend. You heard him. Over and over he kept saying, so many, not enough, so many, not enough."

Max eyeballed Gaz in a way that didn't betray his demeanor to the others, yet sent a clear message any a military man would understand, 'Speak only when spoken to. You aren't helping matters.'

Too late. Gaz had already given Gareth more fuel. Gareth pressed on, "So maybe Caruthers was telling the truth. Maybe he knew they were behind him. Tell me though, how could he have mustered the strength to leave the med hut, or get out of bed for that matter? What about Wizard?"

We all went stone faced with that. Gareth had us where he wanted us.

"Either way, whether they helped him out or dragged him, they're in here now," he said. "We are all educated men," a nasty grin crawled across his face as his eyes shifted toward Jenner, "and women. You can't tell me any different."

Alfie's olive complexion was hitting shades of pale.

"Taft," said Max. "Would you please explain to the gentleman how the motion sensors are wired."

Taft's face lit as if he had been awoken from a spell. "Yeah, certainly. The motion sensors are on their own circuit, separate from the main power, with a redundant local and central back up. Best in the business."

"Same as the cameras?" asked Max.

Taft smiled, relieved by his own realization. "Better actually, because they pull most of the power they need from the solar panels in the field, plus one panel at the top of each section of the fence is dedicated to keeping the batteries charged. You would have to manually shut off each of the detectors one by one, same with the exterior floods, and I am the only one that knows how to do that."

"You see?" said Max.

Alfie was regaining some color. Gareth began to deflate.

"Except," said Taft. His face distorted.

Gareth rejuvenated, "Except what?"

"Wizard," said Taft. "He knows the systems as well as me, I guess."

ELEVEN

The entirety of the Greenhouse was walled and roofed in glass with the exception of the section containing the radio room, labs, and offices. The electrical panels were mounted on the sole solid wall outside of the radio room. Clouds had passed overhead during my time in Agroland, but I don't remember a night so dark. No stars, no moon, only the dull blue glimmer of the cafeteria blanketing the ground beside us, snug against the blackness.

Taft and Hakim each wore a headlamp and held battery operated lanterns. They ran the lanterns up and down the electrical conduits and along the seams of the five boxes.

Lucas and I hovered behind them.

Across the compound, a cone of light washed the back of the water shed.

"Shouldn't there be light back here?" asked Lucas.

"Yeah," said Taft. "We'll get to that. First things first."

Lucas sighed and then asked, "Why are we looking here if you think a pump blew?"

"Well," said Taft. "There are a lot of power units out here. We have half a dozen pumps outside the main door over there," his headlamp swiveled into the direction of the glass doors at the other end of the Greenhouse, "and another dozen over here." The lamp beamed past us, "More back in the field. The central air units you two are leaning on appear to be fine, though. Please don't, by the way."

Lucas and I straightened, the LED beams on the end of our M16s soaring upright.

Taft went on, "And we have another number of electronic motors and monitors on the solar panels. The orchard is full of them, tracking everything from the weather to the growth rate of the date trees, and they all connect back through here." We heard his long screwdriver tapping on the metal of a panel.

"Okay," said Lucas. "I still don't understand why we're looking here."

"Do you smell anything?" asked Hakim.

"Yeah," I said. "Like electric."

"Me too," said Lucas.

"Right," said Hakim. "Electricity actually has no smell. However, electrical arcing splits oxygen molecules that recombine to form ozone, which gives off that sharp, mildly irritating odor."

"Ozone? Heh. That odor is everywhere."

"Yes," said Hakim. Ozone tends to permeate and then hang. The other acrid odor is burnt insulation. Could be anywhere. The night is dark, we can't see, however, whatever blew also knocked out a panel and then cascaded the power."

"A domino effect," said Lucas.

"So we find the panel, we find what blew," I said.

"Precisely," said Taft. "And then we can reset the breakers back up to the main."

Hakim switched his focus back to Taft. "There's no sign of a flare up on the outside of any one of these," he said.

"Huh," said Taft. "And I can't tell if I'm sensing a stronger smell from any one of them. We'll have to open each one."

Taft set down the lantern he had been using to inspect the boxes. He dug his hand into his front pocket and removed a ring of keys. Even out in the desert, there are so many keys. He tilted his head forward sharply to sort the brass and silver in the light, rapidly knocking his thumb against each key until he hit a tiny brass set of five. He flicked up the first and then unlocked the metal box on the end. Taft bobbed his head around to wash the inside of the panel with light. Hakim held up his lantern.

"Everything fine in this one," said Taft.

Taft shut the door and repeated the process with the second and third boxes. When he stuck in the fourth key, the panel door eased open before he turned the lock. Taft's headlamp swung toward Hakim, to us, and then back to the box. "This one is opened," he said.

He flipped the door open with his fingertips. "Would you look at that?"

"Unbelievable," said Hakim.

"Why is the box empty?" asked Lucas.

"That's the question of the day," said Taft. "The entire breaker panel has been ripped clean out."

"How could they know?" asked Hakim.

"What do you mean?" I asked.

"This is the main box, feeds the others," said Taft. "Not so hard to figure out." He lifted his lantern from the ground and held the light below the box. "You see, all of the boxes have a number of conduits, this is the only one with a large pipe. None of the other boxes have that."

"How do we fix the panel?" asked Lucas.

"There is no panel to fix," said Hakim.

"Yeah," said Taft. The light of his headlamp moved up the wall, washing out before reaching the top. "Can one of you shine a light up there?"

Lucas and I pointed of our M16s toward the top of the wall. The beams of our LEDs crisscrossed until Lucas caught a shadow and then we both zeroed in on the same spot. Dangling from the wall by a loose piece of metal was what was left of a camera.

Hakim grunted, and then said, "You better call Max."

TWELVE

Max's response to the sabotage was short. "Keep the channel clear," he said, and that was all.

He was thinking what we all were. Someone could be listening.

Nothing had come over the channel concerning Wizard or our missing guest. Max and Gaz would have either double-timed to the gazebo to rally with Tak and June or were in the process of sweeping the compound one building at a time.

Lucas and I had escorted Taft and Hakim to the Powerhouse to shut down the juice going to the open panel.

Taft again fidgeted with his keys.

The Powerhouse didn't have space for all four of us. Lucas and I waited outside with Hakim as Taft went in. We said nothing to each other while we waited, leaning against the wall away from the edge of the flood. Hakim took our lead. Passing under the lights made you feel exposed. Inside, Taft knocked about whatever was scattered on the workbench. A few moments later, he appeared in the doorway with a wire crate. He set the crate under the light so he could lock the door. The crate held an electrical panel, a mess of breakers, and a tester. The tester was a relic, a needle gauge on a black box with two wires out the top, each tipped with an alligator clip.

The door locked and Lucas broke from the wall. "Let's go," he said, and we were on our way.

Back in the cafeteria, the cooks, Ahmed and Adnan, had popped some microwave popcorn over the gas stove, and a backgammon board was out. Still, the conversations were few. To add a damper on things, the dwarves were praying back in the Greenhouse garden.

Lucas joined Farid and Tyren. Hakim and Taft sat down next to Gareth and Alfie. They set to work on the contents of the crate. The sooner the electrical panel could be fixed, the better for morale.

Jenner was at the edge of the garden, leaning back on a worktable, gazing back into the cafeteria listlessly, her hands clasped and draped to her front. Slack against the table, Jenner was gorgeous as ever. She was the girl you couldn't dress badly. When she locked eyes on me, I walked directly to her, a moth to a flame.

"Okay?" I asked her.

"Yeah," she said. "The dwarves have been praying since you left."

Alfie cleared his throat with an exaggerated, "Hrum."

Gareth rolled his eyes with the burden of having to bear the responsibility of sharing knowledge with the Philistines, "They are reciting verse 255 of the Quran, Ayatul Kursi, the Throne verse."

Alfie kept his head down toward the panel. "They recite the verse for protection from evil."

"That makes sense," I said, my voice low. "Wizard told me they think Caruthers is a Jinn."

"A Jinn. How creative." Gareth sucked in his cheeks, barely tolerant of such an ignorant thought. "That would be fitting. Though I believe they are merely ensuring there will be nothing standing between them and the gates of Paradise." He gave us one of his twisted, half disgusted smiles and then added, "except death."

I turned away from Gareth and Alfie, shrugged my eyes at Jenner, and then mouthed the words, "Excuse me." She did her best to hold back a giggle and then turned away herself.

"Any news?" I asked.

"None," she said. "How about you? Are we going to be able to fix the panel?"

I shrugged, "Taft seems to think so."

Jenner craned her neck, straining to see through the pane of glass into the darkness. "Did you see anything?" she asked.

"You mean anyone," I said.

"Out there," she said. "Anyone, anything."

"No," I said. I gestured toward the glass behind her with a nod. "Maybe Max and Gaz will have something."

Two quads pulled up alongside the glass. Max and Gaz, and they were alone. When they entered through the glass door, Lucas left the table and crossed the room with a water bottle in one hand and popcorn in the other.

Jenner squinted into the darkness toward the parked quads. "Where are Tak and June?"

Gaz shrugged, "Beats all hell. We went out to the gazebo and their gear was there. Quad, blanket, some food and sparkle juice, looked like they were having a picnic."

"And they weren't there?"

"Don't know what to tell you," said Gaz. "Maybe they decided to go for a stroll in the scrub."

"What the hell is that?" said Lucas, his mouth full of

popcorn.

We looked at Lucas. He was staring out into the Agrofield. We followed his eyes. Out in the black, a newly ignited blaze grew into a large ball.

"A bonfire," said Max. "A half a klick out I'd say."

"Yeah," said Lucas.

Max nodded. "Jenner, you have the Greenhouse, whatever blew earlier may have triggered a burn, or—" Max's nod switched to a rocking side to side and he bit into his lower lip.

"Or what?" asked Gaz.

Max scanned the cafeteria to see if anyone else had noticed yet. "Or this could be a distraction, but I'm still not convinced anyone else is in here with us."

"Taft did say there were a lot of electronics out there," said Lucas.

"Right," said Max. "Let's take the quads up the fence and then cut in from the side."

We doubled up onto the two quads, Max and I on one, Gaz and Lucas on the other. Max had a way of instilling confidence in the team. If he thought that the fire was electrical and that there was no danger driving the quads with the lamps on, then so did we. Max had experience we didn't and he led the way, with me on the back of his quad.

In less than a minute, we had booked it up the perimeter parallel to the blaze and were turning to cross the Agrofield. The furrows had the quad bouncing high. Max almost threw me a couple times. My kidneys slammed so hard onto the seat that I was actually glad to finally reach the fire. That is, until we did.

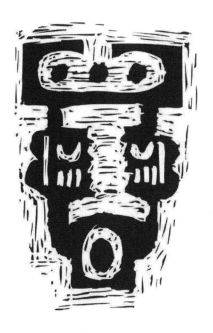

THIRTEEN

The fire was a quarter klick into the crop button, beneath a high arc of the pivot sprinkler. The fire wasn't electrical, or a pump, monitor, or panel. A whole mess of the small olive and date palm orchard had been uprooted, tossed together, and sparked.

Hanging from the metal arm above the blaze was a carcass, and next to the first, another, and then another. The sprinkler was a gallows strung with cadavers, their feet spread and bound to the sides of the triangular trusses the way large game is hung from a gambrel, to be skinned and butchered after the hunt.

After witnessing the worst of war, of death, you would think there would be a part of a man's brain where all of those things could blend, a place where a man could accept any combination as a natural order. There isn't. The hanging cadavers, gutted where they hung, their gleaming innards puddled on the ground beneath them, their flesh peeled away, the oily sheen of their muscle tissue reflecting the fire, slowly dangling game, prepped for the butcher.

All of the missing. All dead, all skinned, except for one. Separated from the others, alone on the end, fully clothed, hand tied, and gagged, was June. Her eyes screamed while her mouth was unable to. Gaz had pulled up first and launched himself over the quad's handlebars to reach her. He lifted her and pulled the gag from her mouth. June was trying to scream even before the gag was free.

The sounds that rattled out of her were a mix of whimpers and gasps.

We were right behind Gaz. Max and I helped Gaz with her weight while Lucas cut her free with the big bone handled blade he always carried.

We eased June onto the ground and then Gaz and Max tried to get her to drink some water. Lucas and I were kneeling down beside June too, but had our M16s in hand, and we were eyeballing the dark the best we could.

Gaz and Max were doing their best too, simply to calm June down. June, the tough as nails wildcat from the Bronx. "All right," said Gaz. "All right, look at me. You need to breathe, soldier."

Soldier, he had said. I never went through any training to prepare me for that. Gaz was on the ball. June locked her eyes with Gaz's. She slowed her breathing. Max offered her more water, and she drank.

"Tell us what happened," said Max.

"He's a monster," said June. "He's unbelievable."

Max offered June another sip. "You mean Caruthers?" June looked at Max funny. He must have remembered she had already left for the Gazebo with Tak when Caruthers awoke. He tried again, "The stranger, you mean the stranger?"

"Yeah," she said. "He grabbed Tak and me and hauled us out here. Picked us up like children. The others were already hanging there. Then he—," she sucked in a bunch of air all at once.

"Killed him, I know," said Max.

"He didn't just kill him, Max, he cut out and ate Tak's heart." June sat up, rubbing her wrists where they were tied, the fire inside her rapidly returning. "He cut out all of their hearts, and then he skinned them. Can you believe that? He skinned every one of them. That's Wizard on the end. And those two are the dwarves. And that's—," she paused, her voice a mix of anger and confusion. "That was Tak."

Max and Gaz said nothing for a long moment. None of us did, we didn't know what to say, I guess. Then Lucas said, "He didn't kill you." Maybe that was supposed to be a silver lining, or maybe a call to arms, because that's what June heard and she wasn't about to be a victim.

"No, he didn't," she said. "He's going to wish he did."

That was right when we heard a rapid burst, carried across the field from the Greenhouse, unmistakably from an M16. Jenner was the only one left in the cafeteria with an M16. Everyone else on the security team, alive and dead, was by the fire in the middle of the Agrofield.

Max keyed his radio, "What's going on?" There was no answer. There was another rapid burst.

We looked toward the Greenhouse, fully visible from out in the Agrofield. The cafeteria glowed vivid, a tiny video screen a half klick away. The screen lit up with another short burst and, even from where we stood, we could see the silhouettes of flailing bodies flying across the cafeteria.

Max made a move toward his quad. "June," he shouted. "We'll be back, we only have room for four." Max punched his electric start and slipped the clutch. Lucas, being the closest to Max, flung himself onto the back of the quad. I climbed on behind Gaz. He was by no means as fast as Max, but we were still on our way lightning quick. I didn't even bother slinging my M16, which became a problem fast. With the mayhem hitting the Greenhouse, we didn't head back to the path by the fence, instead we bee lined to the cafeteria. With only one hand on the sissy bar behind me, I was all over the place. The quad was flying over the young crops, furrows, and irrigation lines that were strewn across the Agrofield. Gaz tossed me and I landed on my face and ate a mouthful of dirt. I also found something hard with my head, a stone, or one of those pumps. I was cut. I felt the blood run down my forehead and wash into my eye. I picked myself up to my knees. Gaz was still going. I was close enough to make out what was happening inside. A tall silhouette lifted someone high over their head, like one of them big time wrestlers, and then effortlessly tossed them far across the cafeteria into the darkness of the Greenhouse garden.

I had a tough time getting to my feet, like I was drunk on whiskey, and when I finally did stand, I fell over again. Then I didn't move. From the direction of the Greenhouse, I heard another short burst followed by a barrage of gunfire. The cavalry had arrived. With a final push to lift myself, I thrust my arms forward against the soil. My head immediately slammed back down, and then nothing.

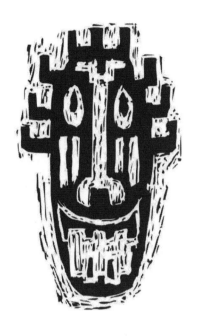

FOURTEEN

I awoke on my face and when I rolled back, the sky was still black. My head throbbed. The whole side of my forehead where I had struck the stone was covered in a sticky sap. The rest of my face was tight in dried blood and caked dirt. I remembered the last time I had tried to stand and was more careful, raising myself to my knees first. The compound was quiet. In the dim lit Greenhouse, there were no silhouettes, no shadows, no movement. Sucking in a deep breath, I pushed myself to my feet. As soon as I was up I was hit with vertigo. I was as nauseous and dizzy as the end of a whiskey drunk.

The desert began to spin and pull out from under me. I had to throw a foot to my side so as not to fall back down, and then I was okay. Farther back in the field, the fire still burned, though not as brightly. There was no movement there either, though at the edge of the firelight, the bodies still hung.

One foot at a time, one in front of the other, I headed to the Greenhouse. My arms hung low by my sides. I noticed that the LED mounted on the end of the M16 had gone out. I slapped the muzzle a couple of times. Nothing. I kept moving.

The walk was quiet, and when I reached the Greenhouse, I almost opened the door and walked right in, like a thousand times before. What was on the other side of the glass stopped me.

I was thankful for the dim blue light. Dark spots covered most every surface, blood that otherwise would have been fruit punch red.

I readied my M16, and then I opened the door.

The cafeteria was in shambles. Every table and chair was overturned. Blood was everywhere. Swaths of blood were smeared on the walls and a few puddles were pooled on the floor. Also on the floor were wide paths of blood from those that had been dragged out to the hallway.

The video panel continued to flip through the tiles of images.

I didn't pay much attention to what was up on the screen. I was more interested in the cases of bottled water stacked by the hallway. The spattered mess on the floor stuck to the soles of my boots as I crossed the room and produced a faint ripping sound with each step. My mouth was dusted, my tongue swollen, and I felt like I was wearing a mask.

Shouldering my weapon, I cracked open a bottle, tilted my head back, opened my mouth and let the water pour, splashing the last bit onto my face. The contents of a second followed the first. I poured the second more slowly so I could use my other hand to wipe and peel off the caked gobs of blood and dirt. I snagged a couple more bottles, stuffed them into my cargo pockets, and then took another to drink.

From across the cafeteria, a low raspy voice asked, "Could you get me one of those?"

My M16 slid from my shoulder to my hands as I spun.

On the floor beyond the cafeteria was Lucas, propped up against the large worktable. He was holding his side.

I had walked right past him.

He tried to say something else and only a cough came out.

"Hold on," I said. I reached back to snag Lucas a water bottle, then went to his aid. The floor smacked as I crossed the room. When I reached the table, I planted myself down so that we were sitting side by side, directly across from the hallway.

I held out the water bottle.

"Thanks," said Lucas. "About time you got here."

"I tripped in the Agrofield." I grinned then pointed to my head, "I bumped my noggin." I flashed a glance to where he held his hand. "Looks like I missed something."

"Yeah," said Lucas. He started to smile and then coughed again. "Caruthers, he's not what you think."

"A terrorist?" I asked.

"He's a terror all right. I emptied a clip and he kept coming. Picked me up like a rag doll and tossed me in here with the hydroponics."

"You gonna be all right?" I asked. I already knew the answer.

"No," said Lucas. "He killed me. Look at this." He lifted his shirt. His belly was soaked with blood. A piece of tubing stuck out of his gut right below his ribcage.

"Hydroponics, I think," said Lucas. "I tried to pull the thing out. Too deep, and when I crawled over here the darn thing worked in deeper. Hurts bad."

"You don't say," I said. "Hey, we'll get you out of here."

"We're not going anywhere," said Lucas. "I'm not, anyway. I would never last a medevac. Besides, Caruthers is coming back for me."

I was sure he was right about the medevac. I didn't know

what he meant about Caruthers. "What are you talking about? I gotta get you over to the med hut."

"I've been sitting here watching the security cameras," he said. "We're safer here right now. He's out there rounding everybody up, one by one."

I looked up at the panel across the room, the mahjong tiles flipping every thirty seconds. Empty areas of the compound filled each square. I didn't understand what Lucas was referring to. Then signs of Caruthers began to appear. A tile on the screen flipped to the garage camera. Beneath the camera was one of the small tractors used for the Agrofield. Hitched to the tractor was a wood sided wagon and inside, stacked on top of each other, were the bodies of the people Caruthers had dragged out of the cafeteria. Some conscious, tied with rope. The women, Maryam, Hannah, and Carver, were silently screaming, half covered beneath the dead bodies Caruthers had thrown onto them.

Images flipped to other parts of the compound and other paths of blood similar to those in the cafeteria. And then there he was, Caruthers. He was wearing security khakis, they must have been Tak's, and a pocketed vest not much different than the one he came in with, most likely from one of the pods. Caruthers was moving with a mission. Lucas and I watched over the next several minutes as he appeared and then disappeared from image to image, going into the buildings and dragging people from where they had tried to hide. Some he pulled out unconscious, dead maybe, others were kicking and screaming.

"How long has he been doing this?" I asked.

"Half hour, hour," said Lucas. "I'm not sure. He seems to know where to look. He sniffs them out."

A large image took the place of two smaller ones in the corner of the screen. The image was from one of the fence top cameras.

"A motion detector kicked on," I said. "Someone is trying to get over the fence."

"Look," said Lucas. "It's Tyren. He's trying to get out."

Additional tiles switched to other nearby motion detectors and the eight small squares became four large ones, each a different angle of Tyren trying to climb the five-meter chain link. Unlike the other security cameras, the motion detector images held and didn't flash off in thirty seconds. We watched Tyren hook his fingers into the chain link to pull himself up. We couldn't hear him, but the agony on his face was unmistakable.

"C'mon," I said. "A little more."

"He needs to hurry," said Lucas. "Those spotlights on the fence make him a sitting duck."

"He's almost there," I said.

At the top of the fence, close up to the camera, Tyren squeezed the razor wire. His hand flew away as he cringed in pain.

"Damn," said Lucas.

Gray scale blood leaked from Tyren's hands and blotted his white button shirt.

"You can do this," I said.

Tyren pulled himself up and with a thrust, threw one leg onto the top of the fence.

"He's going to make it," said Lucas.

Then Tyren's face distorted, like he was about to become ill. His body jerked first once, then twice, then in a rapid jolt he disappeared from the screen, disappeared from all four images. Then the images, one by one, switched back to the smaller tiles. In one was Caruthers, dragging Tyren to the wagon.

"What's he doing," I asked.

"The dead he will put on the fire, the living he will hang," said Lucas. "He will save the women for last."

"Like his story," I said, my eyes focused on the monitor.

Lucas nodded, "Yeah."

"Caruthers has changed," I said. "He looks different."

"He's stronger," said Lucas. "His muscles, his flesh. They're rejuvenating."

I shook my head, "How can that be?"

"My people, the Odawa, have a name for his kind," said Lucas. "They call this creature a Wendigo."

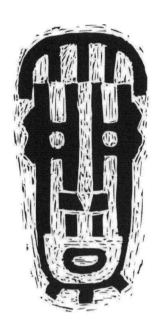

FIFTEEN

Lucas had called Caruthers a creature, not an animal. A creature, a creature his people named Wendigo.

I don't go in for superstition. "The man is obviously a monster," I said. "But he's still a man."

"He might have been once," said Lucas. "He is possessed by an evil spirit. A Manitou that craves, no, not simply craves, has an unending hunger, for human flesh."

"I know what a Wendigo is," I said. "I was raised in the north too. They're no more real than a Sasquatch or Bigfoot."

"Brother," he said. "They're real all right. Look for

67

yourself." Caruthers' image moved from one square on the screen to another. "He is so thin, yet at the same time he is so strong, and look at his eyes, he's hungry. He cannot stop being hungry."

Caruthers' eyes were ghastly. The camera gave them a phosphorescent effect. Still, I didn't understand what Lucas found in them that depicted hunger. So I asked him, "How can you tell?"

"You had a boogeyman when you were a kid?" he asked.

"Don't all kids?" I said. "Mine was under the bed."

"Exactly." Lucas sucked a in a chunk of air. "Your parents probably told you that to keep you in bed."

"Sure," I said. "I guess."

"Well, when I was a boy, my mother—not only her, all the old people—used to scare us from wandering into the woods with stories of monsters and boogeymen. The scariest boogeyman was the Wendigo. Someone possessed for sinning. The possessed were always selfish or gluttons and had, while lost in the woods, been tempted to taste flesh. If a man eats another, even out of necessity for survival, he will be transformed into an evil man-eating Manitou. That's what happened to Caruthers, he became a Wendigo through cannibalism." Lucas was beginning to wheeze as he spoke. Short of breath, he coughed again. I inspected his wound more closely. His lung was collapsing. Lucas gripped my arm. "He's coming," he said.

I turned my attention from Lucas' wound to the video panel.

Caruthers was outside of the Greenhouse.

As he pushed forward on the door on the monitor, the door at the end of the hallway opened inward.

Outside, beneath the cone of light, was Caruthers.

He didn't look the same as he had stretched out in the med hut or up on the monitor. The color of his skin had returned to normal. He was still gaunt, yet no longer desiccated. His long hair seemed a brighter white and his eyes, the large bulbous orbs, glowed ice blue. The unnatural phosphorescence hadn't been an effect of the cameras as I had thought. He actually had the blue eyeshine of a wild animal. When I was a kid, my grandfather had a spotlight on the side of his truck. The light was the kind that you maneuvered by sticking your arm out of the window, like the old police cruisers used to have. He would sometimes drive me out at night to the edge of the woods or a large field and then we would sit in the truck for a while. After some time sitting in the darkness, my grandfather would switch on the spotlight and scan the tree line. There on the edge of the field or among the trees would be the animals he was looking for, deer, coyotes, once I even remember wild dogs. The wild dogs were ferocious predators. They had blue eyeshine.

Caruthers stepped from beneath the floodlight into the shadow of the hallway.

I stopped breathing.

We were sitting on the floor directly in front of the man I'd considered a near corpse a short time before. Lucas had been right. He was coming for us.

Next to me on the floor was my M16. I stretched my fingers toward the weapon.

My mind played hell as the hall leading from the cafeteria to the door stretched out and then came back like a rubber band. I was breathing again and my deep breaths were the cause of the illusion. Maybe that's what a panic attack is because I noticed all of a sudden my heart was beating a thousand times a minute. I could feel the pounding up in my throat. Every time the hallway stretched, Caruthers would slide away and then pop closer than he was before, his long hair snow white, and his glowing eyes ice blue.

When my fingers reached my M16, my mind instantly soothed. Having your hand on your weapon is calming when there is a psycho killer bearing down on you. I eased the weapon close with as much stealth as I could muster. I measured Caruthers' pace, and waited for him to close in. I wanted a swift draw and a sure mark.

A few steps short of the cafeteria, Caruthers stopped. His

hand lifted slowly from his side. I squeezed the pistol grip of the M16, ready to pull and shoot, in case that hand held a weapon. Caruthers didn't draw a weapon. He reached his raised hand to the side of the hallway and pressed lightly on a door. The slow creak told me that the lab door, hidden from my view, was swinging open. When the creaking ceased, Caruthers twisted to face the lab. He didn't enter. He stood there silent in the dark hallway.

Never before had I noticed the white noise that echoed off the glass panes of the Greenhouse. The aeration bubblers in the aquaponic trout tanks fizzed loudly and the water that trickled through the thin aggregated tubes that sprouted the strawberries became a waterfall.

On the monitor, Caruthers had moved from image to image, building to building, fluidly, without hesitation, but I didn't catch his every move, or see him actually kill anyone. He was out of frame when Tyren was torn from the fence. Perhaps before each kill he stood as he did in the shadow of the hall. His face was too shadowed to show expression, if he wore one. For the first time, I noticed how tall Caruthers was, easily over two meters. He had appeared tall in his hospital bed and on the monitor, but I had given that to how frail he had become from the desert, the thinness exaggerating his height. He had appeared lanky and willowy. He was neither anymore. He was solid. There was enough light in the shadow of the hallway to see that his neck and wrist, each as thin as reeds in the med hut, had gained girth.

After a long moment of standing sentinel in front of the lab, Caruthers' head dropped to the side, and then tilted slightly back, an animal focusing on a scent. Then with sudden determined force, he sprung into the lab and disappeared from our view.

Neither Lucas nor I said anything. To quell the stillness, I continued to focus on the sounds of the Greenhouse, the hydroponics above and the aquaponic tanks behind, and then, from inside the lab, came the sound of a young man singing. I thought he was singing because he spoke the words in Arabic and had started softly, repeating them over and over and then began to escalate in volume and intensity so they sounded musical. Then I recognized that he was repeating a mantra. I also recognized the voice. The man in the lab was Farid, the Saudi consultant. I could hear the mantra clearly, "A-ozu billahi mena shaitaan Arrajeem, A-ozu billahi mena shaitaan Arrajeem." I understood the meaning of this Muslim phrase. The phrase was one used when felt unsafe, scared by something. The phrase roughly translated meant, 'I seek refuge in Allah from the cursed Satan.'

I remembered what Wizard had said about Satan being a Jinni. Satan, Jinni, Genie, Wendigo, desert crazed psycho killer, labels didn't matter. Farid was repeating the mantra over and over, louder and louder, and then, his words were abruptly replaced by what I can only describe as a gurgle. A loud crushing gurgle followed by a crack, a loud snap that hung in my mind as the heavy silence returned to that end of the Greenhouse. I stared toward the empty hallway and waited for the inevitable. From within the lab I heard equipment fall and something heavy being shoved to the side. Then Caruthers returned to the hall, dragging Farid, limp behind him. Caruthers didn't stop outside the door of the lab. He didn't turn to face the two of us on the floor across the room. He kept moving toward the door at the end of the hallway, to exit the Greenhouse the way he had come.

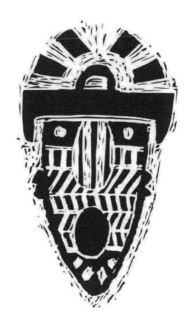

SIXTEEN

Caruthers had come to the Greenhouse as Lucas said he would, in search of a body to take with him. We didn't anticipate there was another hiding in the Greenhouse, closer to the door than us. Our pure luck seemed to be that Caruthers was working on a first come first serve basis.

"We have to get out of here," I said. "He'll be back."

"He'll be back for me," said Lucas. "You have to go."

Even in the dull light, Lucas was noticeably losing color.

"Hold on," I said bringing myself to my feet. "You still have your light?"

"Yeah," said Lucas. He raised the muzzle of his M16 up to me so that I could unsnap the small light. I dialed the lumens down to a dull glow and then went over to the supply cabinets beneath one of the other tables. After shuffling through a few items, I found the suitcase sized first aid kit.

I scurried back to Lucas and then cracked open the case. The kit was well stocked with saline, antiseptic sprays, antibiotic wipes, medicines, ointments, bandages of all types, and even a defibrillator. I sorted through the compact boxes of drugs until I found the one I was looking for, the one labeled fentanyl. I ripped open the box. Inside were a half dozen plastic sticks with a hard candy on the end. We called the sticks morphine lollipops. They weren't morphine, the painkiller fentanyl was much more powerful. I pulled one out for Lucas. His eyes met mine defiantly. I sensed he was wavering. He was obviously in great pain and the fentanyl would fix that. The tradeoff would be his clarity and reaction time. He must have decided he was already compromised, because in the end, he gave me a nod and took the lollipop from me. He sucked hard and took in some deep breaths through his nose. The painkiller must have worked fast because he didn't so much as flinch when I began bandaging his side.

The adrenalin from Caruthers' visit to the cafeteria was doing a job on me. No longer disoriented and loopy, I was ready to go. After I taped up Lucas, I took a minute to pour some saline on my forehead and fixed myself up as well.

Lucas and I didn't speak while I played medic. I'm sure the fentanyl drew him away a little but he could not have escaped the reality that Caruthers could be coming back any second. When I finished with the kit, I slapped Lucas on the shoulder.

"All right, that's good enough," I said. "Let's radio for help and then book it out of here."

Lucas slowly met my eyes. "No," he said. "You go. Get some help if you can."

I didn't argue. Moving him twice was a bad idea. I decided I would radio for help and then come back and take him out the door I had come in. I was only going for a minute but I didn't know when Caruthers was coming back. I offered Lucas a clip and he shook his head. "No, no," he said. He reached to his side and fumbled with his knife. I helped him unsheathe the bone handled blade and, with my hand on his, he pulled the large knife up to rest on his chest. He closed his eyes and sucked in another deep breath.

I squeezed his hand. "You gonna be okay?" I asked.

He bobbed his head in a few short nods. He tried to speak but had to clear his throat. "Hrum. Yeah," he said. "Go ahead, get help, I'm fine."

"I'll be back in a minute," I said. He was already fading.

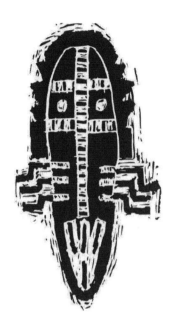

SEVENTEEN

The radio room was steps from the still wide open door Caruthers had used when he came to take Farid.

My adrenalin was pumping, but as I stepped across the dark sticky pools, my legs threatened to carry me the other way. The hallway was the worst. The bodies Caruthers had collected from the cafeteria had all been drug down the narrow corridor. There were no edges to creep upon without that layer of dark ooze sucking at my feet. Each step pulled away like a piece of tape. I would have been smarter to pick up my pace but the idea that Caruthers' tall lank figure could fill the doorframe at any second hindered my progress. The closer I came to the doorway the more well-lit the hall became. Bloody claws marks lined the walls near the floor from those that continued to fight, the women on the wagon.

When I reached the radio room, I bumped the door open with my elbow so that I could back in with my weapon still pointed toward the light.

The inside of the radio room was humming from the small fans cooling the electronics and was filled with a dim hue, similar to the cafeteria. A desk, lined with video panels, sat across from the door. A screensaver of floating album covers provided the dull light in the room. The other screens were dark. Little blue and green lights dotted the metal boxes below the desk. These were the backup units and computer workstations. Apart from two chairs at the desk, the only furniture in the room was Wizard's bunk on one side wall and a metal shelving unit stocked with electronics on the other. We called this room by a few names, the radio room, the signal shop, the com center. The reality was that there was no radio. Everything that Wizard used was on one computer or another. The large monitor with the floating screensaver was the one we used to make video calls home. The mic and camera were built in, all I had to do was turn on the software.

I backed toward the desk, my M16 solidly square with the door, and then awkwardly reached behind me to tap the keyboard. The room suddenly became far brighter. The light caused my heart to pump even faster. I was hesitant to turn toward the screen. There was no window to that room, still I felt like I had lit a beacon. Since Caruthers hadn't lunged into the doorway, I took a breath and turned to the screen. The image on the monitor calmed me, if only for a split second. Two naked women filled the display, side by side in a seductive pose. I remembered that Wizard had been fastening his pants when he came to relieve my watch. I hit the escape key and then maneuvered the mouse to the icon I needed. Facing the door, I had a hard time with the mouse, so I spun toward the computer to open the video caller program. I appeared in a window on the screen. My face shadowed in the dim light. My face was smeared with antiseptic ointment, dirt, and blood. The bandage I had taped to my head was thick and puffy, still not a bad job considering I put the thing on myself. To the side of my face was a column of names. I double tapped the first on the list, the equivalent of our security hotline. A disc spun in the center of the screen and hung there for what seemed like forever. I faced the door again and kept looking back at the screen waiting for somebody else's face to fill the camera window.

After what seemed an eternity, the disc stopped spinning, and a box popped up with the words, 'unable to connect'. I clicked on the next name down, a hospital line for emergency medicine. The disc spun and the box reappeared. I clicked the next, and the next, even a name designating a refugee camp up near the Syrian border. None of them were able to connect. Each attempt had taken minutes, minutes that together had to be close to a half an hour, maybe more, maybe less. I can't say what was wrong with the com line. I wasn't trained on any other. My guess is, that probably didn't matter. I gave up and decided to haul Lucas out of there.

My legs cooperated a whole lot better coming out of that radio room and back down the hall toward Lucas. When I reached him, I clutched his arm. "C'mon," I said. "I'll carry you."

Lucas had the pungent scent of urine. He had pissed himself. I took a knee to check his pulse. He was limp, pale, and dead. I had taken too long. My guess is that probably didn't matter either.

With the radio out, I had no distinct plan other than putting some space between myself and Caruthers. He appeared on the monitor. He was in the garage, looming in and out of view. I thought about sneaking past him to the SUV and didn't like the math. I thought about making a run out the door toward the gate and couldn't. He was between me and the gate, between me and everything on the other side of the cafeteria.

Out in the field, the fire still burned. I remembered what he said about the bodies on the fire. He would be taking that wagon out there. All I had to do was wait him out. When he went out to the field, I would hop in the SUV and that was that.

The Greenhouse didn't feel all too safe. Caruthers had already been there a few times collecting and could decide to head back for Lucas. I wasn't going to take a chance of waiting for him there.

I left by the glass door to the Agrofield, the way I had come in.

I stuck to what little plan I had, to put some space between myself and Caruthers. The safest place to be was where he wasn't, out into the Agrofield under the cover of darkness.

To avoid the risk of my backlit silhouette drawing him to me, I circumvented the still burning fire by way of the fence. Motor memory kicked in once I set foot on the little road that ran the perimeter. There was no horizon in the distance, no depth to the dark. Countless perimeter patrols kept me going forward without wavering too close to the perimeter. A step too near the fence would set off the motion detectors and click on the lights.

There would have been no difference if I were to have walked with my eyes closed, which suited me fine. I didn't look back toward the Greenhouse until I was well past that hellhole of a fire. From the arc of the sprinkler, the bodies still hung, tangerine and crimson in the light of the low burning fire. Keeping my head forward, I trudged a full klick through the darkness before cutting across the Agrofield toward the outer patch of solar panels.

My plan was to maneuver far across the field to the solar panels, wait for Caruthers to move to the fire, and then beeline toward the gate. Cautiously, I crept across the field, unable to find a path, bumping into trees and stumbling over pumps. Finally, I reached the outer patch of solar panels. No longer moving forward, the cover of darkness became an abyss and I started to become anxious. Leaning against the side of a panel,

I opened one of the water bottles I'd brought from the cafeteria and guzzled down half. Back toward the compound was the fire, the glow of the Greenhouse, and the single cone of light at the door of the water shed. That was the way out, past the water shed. The warm solar panel at my back and the drink of water had soothed me. Shifting my shoulder into the panel, I slid around and away from the buildings so that I was flat against the small wall. The solar panels were easy to hide behind. So I hid, and then I waited.

EIGHTEEN

I didn't have to wait long before I heard the idle rumble of the small tractor across the crop button. The engine revved and clucked hard as she shifted into gear.

I pivoted around to the side of the solar panel to get a peek at the compound. There, near the single light of the water shed, two tiny dots sprayed amber as the tractor turned out toward the Agrofield.

He was coming.

The fire was a half klick away from where I knelt, the garage another half a klick. I watched the little eyes of light bobble through the darkness in a slow and definite course toward the fire.

All I needed to do was slip past Caruthers while he was distracted at the fire.

Hunched low, with the water shed light as a beacon, I began to head back toward the compound, the SUV, and the gate.

I had already gone half a klick, the bonfire was a hundred meters to my left, and Caruthers was almost there. All I had to do was keep moving forward and I would be free to find help. Another fifteen minutes and I would be a few klicks away. Hovering behind the headlights, I noticed glints of red. The wagon, or the tractor for that matter, was hidden in darkness, so I guessed the red was from the reflectors tacked to the wagon's wooden sides. The wagon that held the bodies of people I had lived beside, ate with, laughed with. Tyren and Farid were in that wagon. On the monitor in the cafeteria, Maryam, Hannah, and Carver were still alive and we had left June at the bonfire. The thought of them still alive taunted me. If I escaped the compound alone I would not be helping them at all. There would be no rescue, only recovery. If I could save any one of them from Caruthers, pull them from his view, out into the darkness, they may have a chance.

Hunching down, I pulled my M16 close to my chest. I looked at the fire, the lights of the tractor, the light on the water shed, the tractor, the water shed. I am embarrassed to say that there was a dilemma, but there was. I kept looking between the water shed and the headlights. While I weighed my options, the headlights continued to bob up and down over the furrowed crop button. In the dark, the two lamps may well have been those of a tugboat trolling to shore, up and down and forward. I thought again about those that were still alive.

Never did I have an issue going into danger. Sure, I had been scared quite a few times when I was active. Afraid of being shot or stepping on something that would end me. This was different, an instinctual fear. I sucked in another deep breath and willed my legs to a new course, toward the fire.

The fire was low from burning untended over the last hour or two, so the Agrofield was cloaked in darkness. That was good. Except for the wheeled metal struts that supported the sprinkler, there was nothing to hide behind in the crop button. Careful to stay out of range of what little firelight there was, I sprinted the few meters between each strut. I picked a spot with a good vantage to watch Caruthers, a safe distance, yet close enough to make a move either toward a rescue, or to flee.

The little lights floated toward the fire circle and then, as if pulled from a veil of darkness, the little orange tractor appeared with the wooden wagon behind. Up on the seat, his snow white hair brightened by firelight, was Caruthers.

He pulled the small tractor to a spot across the fire from where I watched and then parked in front of a pile of small trees he had already gathered from the orchard. He went right to work moving the trees onto the fire. They were green and slow to ignite, at first creating a great cloud of smoke that briefly masked the fire and darkened the Agrofield. All at once, the dried leaves began to crackle.

I tried to make myself smaller, more hidden, as the blaze grew. After throwing all of the uprooted trees he had gathered onto the fire, Caruthers went around to the back of the wagon. His movements were mechanical and his deformity lank, tall, unnatural, a hideous puppet. One by one, he effortlessly lifted each of the dead over to the bonfire and threw them in, tossed them as one would toss a bale of hay or firewood. The corpses were toys to him. He didn't even seem to flex, his strength so immense. Other bodies, those he had bound with rope, he dropped to the side. They were still alive.

Caruthers threw eight bodies to the ground, six to the fire.

Lucas had been the first to go in. He had been on the top of the pile, the last added to the wagon. I was reassured I had done the right thing by hiding in the field. The next corpse would have been my own. Of the other five in the fire, I could only make out the faces of Taft and Alfie. Poor old Alfie, I am sure he had no chance, then again, none of them did.

After Caruthers emptied the wagon, he hauled a large

plastic fuel container from the back of the tractor and, with wide swings of his arms, hurled streams of the liquid onto the flames. Sparks and flame erupted, igniting what hadn't already begun to burn. The long palm leaves near the edge of the fire crackled loudly. Caruthers held the container up over his head and came to life. He danced a high-kneed jig. Then he tossed the fuel can aside and turned to face the living bound on the ground. His hands were to his waists, his elbows out, and chest up. He was still gaunt, yet seemed more muscular.

In the fire, the bodies burned. Flesh boiled and peeled away from muscle. Cracks and pops, indistinguishable from flesh or wood, jarred the Agrofield and then the smell came, meat cooking.

Farid was the first to be hung from his feet. He dangled there without resistance, followed by Sam, she was a botanist, then the rest, eight of them in all. None made a movement, yet I figured since they weren't tossed in the fire, they must still be alive.

NINETEEN

A trancelike state had come over me. When I felt the slight touch to my shoulder, I almost gave my position away. I swung my M16 around ready for blunt force. A hand forced the muzzle down and another slapped across my mouth.

Crouched above me in the shadowy light was June.

She placed a finger over her mouth. Then in a soft whisper she said, "I have the quad."

"What quad?" I asked.

"From the gazebo," she said.

That made sense. June and Tak must have taken the quad

out there to begin with.

Peering into the black behind her, I asked, "Where?" Meaning where was the quad.

Subtly she gestured that she had been pushing the quad around the fire when she found me. My silhouette again had given me away. She shrugged and whispered, "What happened?"

The roar of the blaze drowned out our voices. Still, I told her what I could with as few words as possible.

"And the rest of the team?" she asked.

"Lucas is dead," I said. "The others..." I shrugged and shook my head.

June and I kept our eyes fixed on Caruthers. Having finished hanging those that had been bound on the ground, he went back to the wagon. We had thought, I had thought, the wagon was empty. I was wrong. I recognized her as soon as he lifted her out. She was the only one I had seen conscious. Gagged, tied, and writhing wildly, Jenner was still putting up a fight.

The adrenalin my body had pumped through me before must have dulled, because the new surge had me bursting from my skin. I think I used a single breath when I told June, "We have to help her."

"Hold on," said June. "There is nothing we can do. Believe me. He's too strong."

"We have to do something," I said.

"Yeah," said June, even after her traumatic stint hanging from the sprinkler, she was the voice of reason. "We have to get the quad. One of us can be the gunner while the other drives."

June may have said something else. I didn't hear her.

With one arm, Caruthers hung Jenner from the sprinkler. Her body convulsed as she tried desperately to wriggle free from her restraints. Indifferent to struggle, Caruthers ripped away the front of her shirt. Jenner's large breasts, sweaty from her fight, gleamed in the firelight. Caruthers pulled a large blade from his side, Lucas' long bone handled blade.

Caruthers wrapped his long bony finger around one of her breasts. Jenner's muffled screams cut through her gag as he groped her. Slowly he squeezed his claw of a hand, his head tilting in sick pleasure while Jenner's nostrils flared with sobs.

Then in a flash, Caruthers raised the arm wielding the knife and brought the blade down to her chest. With that single stroke, he hacked away her breast. A loud curdling, muffled scream escaped her, and then she was silent. She had passed out.

In that moment, the other women hanging beside her began to sway, trying to escape. Maybe Jenner's screams woke them or maybe they had simply been playing possum. Either way, Caruthers ignored them. He held Jenner's amputated breast up, the skin cupped where he had groped her, the raw flesh exposed. Then, his glowing eyes wide, he bit into the flesh like a melon.

June had been holding me back, her arm around my neck, her ass anchoring her down. That was not enough. No longer able to bear watching, I launched up. From deep down in my gut a came a sound like none I ever made, a war cry.

In a full run, I went for Caruthers.

He lifted his eyes from the bloody melon, lazily glanced in my direction, and then opened his mouth wide and again brought his long white teeth into his sample of Jenner's raw flesh.

From the other side of the fire, behind the wagon, came another war cry. "Now!" yelled Max. Why he hadn't made a move before is beyond me. Maybe he had the same common sense as June and wouldn't have made a move at all. Whether he had planned the attack or not, I initiated battle, so there he was, and Max wasn't alone. Gaz was by his side, as were Hakim and Gareth. They stormed Caruthers and, much closer to him than I had been, waved me from the line of fire. That was fine with me. Not missing a stride, I veered toward Jenner to cut her down.

Caruthers was not as dismissive with the gang of four as he had been to me. He threw the lump of flesh he had held down to the ground and charged. There were a lot of muzzle flashes at once. I could not distinguish which shots connected. Not one of the bullets dropped Caruthers. He initially jerked back from the force of the first few and then, as Lucas had described, kept coming.

Gaz was the first to physically engage. With the same effort you would swat at a fly, Caruthers dispatched him with the back of his hand, snapping the young Brit's neck on contact. Gaz' head flopped unnaturally back and to the side while his body flew up and onto the tractor. In that split second Gaz was airborne, his body reacted to the blow by tensing, causing his hand to squeeze the trigger of his M16. A rapid burst released across the hanging survivors.

The M16s Gareth and Hakim were auto firing might as well have been cap guns. Impressively, they held their ground until their clips were drained, and then used the rifles as clubs. Caruthers took two long strides toward Hakim. Hakim swung the M16 around from the muzzle and thwacked Caruthers with the butt of the weapon. Caruthers absorbed the blow, then with lightning agility, clutched the M16 in his claw grip before Hakim could pull the weapon back to swing again. He cast the rifle aside. Hakim had a crazy, surprised look on his face, even more so when Caruthers took hold of him like a rag doll. Hakim's surprise relented to a scream as he was lifted over Caruthers head, and heightened to a howl as he flew into the bonfire. I'd like to think the fall into the flames knocked him out.

Flanking Caruthers, Max clutched the monster's arm and spun him around. Max had Caruthers attention. Caruthers bent his knees and arched forward, holding his arms out to his side like a bear. Max mirrored him.

The two began to circle, throwing jabs at each other. Max eased close enough to land a series of rapid punches square into the middle of Caruthers face and then faded back. Another half circle and Max repeated the maneuver. Caruthers' head bobbed back with every blow. He appeared unable to defend himself against the master soldier. He threw a few jabs at Max, not one connected.

Caruthers continued to circle, his arms began to drop, his step became uneasy, and then, his balance fading, he began to sway. The punches to his head were taking a toll.

Max went in for a third time to finish him off. When Max closed in, Caruthers surprised him by grabbing his forearms with the same lightning speed that had stripped Hakim of his weapon. He regained his balanced stature.

Sardonic is a word I learned in school. Sardonic means 'grimly mocking.' That's what Caruthers was doing to Max. That's the best way to describe his expression, except, at the angle they were to me, almost across the fire, but not, Caruthers' sardonic expression was exaggerated.

At first Max showed determination, resistance. Then Caruthers crushed his forearms. Max clenched his teeth. There was a series of cracks. Max went to his knees. With those bony bare hands, Caruthers was able to squeeze so hard the arms broke.

The look of fear across Max's face was one I'd never thought possible.

Once Caruthers had Max to his knees, he released his forearms. Max's arms were broken, bent, and indented where he had held them. Max peered up at him, dazed. Caruthers calmly clasped his fingers behind Max's head, almost maternally. He peered into Max's eyes. The exchange could have been mistaken for one of mercy or even pity for the mere mortal that had the nerve to challenge him. As Caruthers eyes widened I realized he was toying with Max. He wanted to be sure that Max clearly understood what was to happen next. Without taking his eyes away from Max's own, Caruthers drew his long clasped hands together so that his palms rested on the sides of Max's skull. And then, with the same slow steady force he'd used on the forearms, he squeezed.

Max did nothing. He hadn't understood what was happening. Perhaps the thought of defeat simply could not register. When he did realize what was happening to him, his entire body began to quiver and shake. His awareness that he was a small mouse trapped in the paws of a large cat came too late. The pressure increased until Max's skull was as crushed and as broken as his arms. His eyes, expressed from their sockets, dangled onto his cheeks.

Rather than toss Max aside, Caruthers held the dead soldier in his hands, even after his death. He inspected the mutilated warrior that had dared to challenge him, satisfied with his handy work. Then he turned his attention to Gareth and me.

TWENTY

Caruthers was still a few meters away, across the large body-filled bonfire from where I knelt next to Jenner. She was still out, she hadn't moved or whimpered since I'd pulled her from the sprinkler. I wasn't sure if she was alive or dead.

During the fight between Max and Caruthers, Gareth had travelled the long way around the fire and was now by my side.

There was no doubt in our minds as to what was to occur next. Caruthers had disposed of Gaz, Hakim, and even Max with little effort and now his sights were set on us.

The monster titled his head from one side to the next, the

flesh near his mouth so eroded I thought maybe he was smiling at us.

The chainsaw whine of a quad engine filled the Agrofield. Gareth and I both turned toward the bobbing headlights cutting through the darkness, rushing toward the fire.

June had gone to the quad. Rather than fleeing, she was coming in like the cavalry.

Caruthers, fixed on his prey, paid no attention to the lights in the field behind us. I guess he didn't consider us a threat because he was in no hurry. Hands by his sides, he began to casually walk toward us.

Kneeling the way I was, there wasn't much more I could do other than let my M16 drop from my shoulder, point the muzzle into his direction, and squeeze the trigger. My M16 was set to automatic and I wasn't prepared for the rapid burst. I was almost knocked back on my ass. Somehow by freak accident I managed to do what no one else had. I had sent that entire burst directly into Caruthers' head.

Caruthers hovered for a few seconds, and then dropped to the dirt.

The quad rolled up next to us. June launched herself from the seat. "You got him," she said as she went to free Hannah, the closest dangling survivor. "I was beginning to think bullets couldn't take the monster down."

"The head shot was sufficient enough," said Gareth. Then he helped June lower Hannah to the ground.

"Yeah," I said. "But how many times did you hit him alone?"

"There was probably so much morphine in his system that he did not have the sense to drop, or something else maybe," said Gareth. "Pump a man full of enough PCP and he'll keep fighting with his limbs blown off."

I put my fingers to Jenner's neck to check for a pulse. "She's still alive."

"We need to get her out of here," said Gareth.

"We're all getting out of here," said June. She released the rope gag from around Hannah's head. "I don't care how tight we squeeze into the SUV."

Gareth was already tending to Maryam. "She's dead," he said.

"They were all shot," I said. "By Gaz. I think they are all dead."

June put her hand behind Hannah's head to help her with a sip of water. I watched Hannah lean forward to drink. Her eyes spread wide and she screamed. I looked up as that long skinny arm brought the blade of the bone handled knife from high above June's shoulder down into Hannah's chest. With his other hand, he grabbed June by the hair, jerked his arm back, and snapped her neck. He was so fast and moved so fluidly. Caruthers had risen, his shadowed face rejuvenated and merely marred with lesions where the bullets had struck him.

My M16 was on the ground next to me. I lifted the weapon and again pointed the muzzle at Caruthers. In a lashing motion, Caruthers pulled the blood covered blade from Hannah's chest and then threw the knife in my direction.

I was not his target.

Jenner caught Lucas' knife in the chin. The metal sank deep into her skull.

I squeezed the trigger and nothing happened. The M16 was jammed.

Caruthers could have taken either one of us right then. He didn't even stand. The bodies of the freshly killed women were what he wanted. After he threw the knife, he went to work tearing away June's shirt.

Gareth screamed. "We have to go!" He dragged me by my collar to my feet and toward the quad. Taking hold of the handlebars, I punched the ignition button and pulled my leg over. Gareth and I became a four-legged animal. He was glued to my back, climbing onto the quad with me. With both of his hands, he slapped my shoulders and screamed, "Go! Go, you fool!"

As we fled, Caruthers was squatting beside June, sinking his teeth into her breast.

TWENTY-ONE

Caruthers had mentioned the Anthropophagi. You wouldn't think I would remember a word like that. I do. Gareth had said the Anthropophagi were an ancient tribe from the west of the Ethiopian Kingdom. They were also referred to as the Man-eaters because their diet consisted of human flesh.

Gareth had said that the Man-eaters were a myth and Caruthers had corrected him. Regardless of name, Caruthers had said, they were quite real.

We had thought, at least I thought, that Caruthers was

delusional. We were so wrong. He was a man-eater, a cannibal, yet something more. The dwarves identified him right off, they called him a Jinni, and then Lucas called him a Wendigo. Farid had called him Satan.

Whatever Caruthers was, he was not a man.

Gareth must have been thinking the same because as soon as I drove the quad into the garage, he said as much. Beneath the camera light, where the trailer had been, was a pool of blood. He was peering at that pool and the punch colored trail that led out of the garage into the darkness when he said to me, "Akers. We have to kill that thing."

"I tried that already," I told him. The light on the end of my muzzle, the one Lucas had given me, flared bright as I adjusted the lumens. I set the beam wide and then scanned the garage. A force of habit, I ran the beam along the sides of the SUV. Everything appeared normal.

"Did you see me unload on him?" I asked as I went over to the driver's door. "His face grew back."

The phrase, 'His face grew back' was one I never thought I would hear myself say, but that is exactly what I said. And when the words left my lips, so matter of fact, the crazy events of the past few hours played back in my mind in numbing clarity, a slow motion reel of a long train derailing, one mangled car at time.

As I reached for the handle of the SUV, Gareth grabbed my arm. The flashlight was fixed to the end of the rifle, though I'm not sure if he put that together when the beam hit his face. Whether I meant to point the muzzle or the light I am not even sure, though I was ready to lay him out. The look on his face stopped me. Gareth wasn't being condescending or dictatorial. He wasn't trying to push me around. He was sincerely concerned.

"The only way to ensure Caruthers dies," he said, "is by blowing him into fragments."

I sighed. "Yeah." Then I lowered the barrel and shook my head. "That's a super idea. So is driving out through that gate." I tried to mirror Gareth's expression, forgetting my blood and dirt smeared face was hidden behind my light. He let go of my arm and stood silent as I opened the door to the SUV. I handed him the large light from the pocket of the door so that he would have one of his own.

The key, as always, was in the ignition. I reached in and cranked the key forward a full turn. Nothing happened.

He watched me turn the key a few more times and when I slammed my hand against the steering wheel, he said, "It's not going to start."

The frustration was obvious in my voice. "And how do you know that, Professor?"

"Do you really believe he would've left us a way out?" he asked. In a kind way though, without the sarcasm I was so used to.

I had to ask, "What do you mean?"

Gareth shrugged, "We have never heard of him."

I rolled my eyes. "And?"

Gareth reminded me of Caruthers' own story. "He said he has been with others before us. If anyone had ever survived and gotten away, we would have heard something, or somebody would have."

I gotta give Gareth credit, he was right. Serial killers don't travel too far if they leave survivors behind, even out in the desert. Still, I had to pop the hood of the engine compartment to have a look for myself. His suspicion was confirmed. The battery was missing. We searched the SUV and garage. The spare in the back compartment was also missing, as were the two that should have been on the back wall shelf.

A battery, something so basic and simple, yet out in the middle of nowhere, a treasure.

Gareth was rubbing his chin again, and of course, his cheeks were sucked in. Even in the dim light, that guy couldn't hide a thought process. That was exactly where he usually became a jerk. That time he wasn't. "I can rig the smaller one from the quad," he said. "That will at least be enough to start the SUV. We will have to run light, that's all. No air conditioning, maybe no headlights."

Nodding in agreement I said, "All right." His plan was better than any I had. The batteries could have been a meter outside the door, yet the odds of us finding anything in the dark were nil. "What can I do to help?"

He gestured up. "You can go up on the roof to watch for Caruthers."

"Yeah," I said. "I can do that."

He reached into the SUV and brought out one of the two-way radios from the console. He switched channels away from those by the fire before he bothered to turn the device on to check for power. The two-way was fine. "I will also rig the fuel containers to blow," he said. "The timing will be close." He keyed the device and then rocked his head from side to side. "I can detonate them remotely when he closes in."

After agreeing to Gareth's plan, I jogged to the far end of the Greenhouse and entered through the glass door I had used before. I climbed up to the catwalk used to access the hydroponics, and from there went to the roof. The Greenhouse roof gave me a good vantage point to the field and the compound. The sky was so dark I could walk upright with no risk of being discovered. The tower, of course, would have fulfilled the purpose, but was also a trap if Caruthers came too close. From the top of the Greenhouse, I could escape in any direction.

The entire time from when I rounded the corner of the Greenhouse, entered the glass door, climbed all the way up the ladder, and onto the roof, I kept one eye out toward the field. The bonfire was still burning bright, the tractor was still parked, and the bodies were still hung. The tall, lanky Caruthers appeared to be peeling away their clothes. I couldn't remember how many we had left hanging and I didn't stop to do a count.

The advantage of height let me see more lit ground. That is how I spotted Caruthers when he left the bonfire minutes later. He was heading toward the Greenhouse across the pale blue carpet of light cast out by the security panel in the cafeteria. He had finished whatever he was doing by the fire and was coming for us. That hair of his grew whiter the closer he came. I thought about making a break to warn Gareth and then I remembered that the same panel that was lighting the Agrofield displayed the images from the garage camera. If Caruthers caught Gareth and I on the screen, he could easily get the drop on us.

I guess I had a whole lot of courage or a mess of stupid because I decided the best thing to do was to distract him. So before he reached the Greenhouse I yelled down, "We figured you out." Caruthers stopped walking. I continued, "You told us some spook story to throw us off and then shut down the power."

Caruthers' face was hidden by the night and for that I was thankful. He was still too far to make out any more detail than his figure. A few seconds passed where he stood silent. He must have been scanning the rooftop to pinpoint where I was. Then, the monster that had been more machine than man began to speak. The voice that had been so dry and raspy had changed, silky and with much more strength. He sounded like a much younger man. Even his accent was more defined. With the limited light, I would have believed another man altogether was standing in the Agrofield.

"Yes," he said. "I did spin the tale a tad. Sven and I were hunters, poachers actually. We were in the north with some hired hands that turned out to be a ruthless bunch. There was a mutiny of sorts. Our own porters sabotaged our vehicles to hijack the expedition. We were lucky to escape them, but then we had to travel on foot through the bush. Sven was wounded. There had been a drought that year, so food was scarce. Sven and I began to starve." Caruthers paused. "Have you ever felt that?" he asked.

I didn't answer. I wasn't about to give him any more of a bearing on where I was.

After another pause, he continued. "Well, we were hunters. So I went out to hunt. I finally came upon a young warrior. I approached him and asked if he knew where the animals had gone. The young warrior attacked me, and I killed him, barely.

Self defense, my life or his. What happened next was," he paused again, "let's say, transformative. You see, I was very hungry, had not eaten in days, and there were no animals to be found. I was famished, ravenous you might say, and there before me was fresh meat. In a fit of starvation, I field dressed the young lad and ate his heart. I brought the rest of the meat back. I told Sven the meat was gazelle. Sven was too far-gone to eat. I made him a broth. The meat was not enough for me, though. I could not satiate myself. The next night I killed Sven and ate him as well, and then I went out into the darkness and came across the documentary expedition. I killed the members of the party most likely to cause trouble and then tied the others." Caruthers began to slowly walk toward the Greenhouse. "You now," he said, as casually as conversing over tea. "In Western Kenya, long ago, during times of war or in the event of famine, the women were often forced to slice off a part of their fatty bodies to feed the warriors. The three women in the expedition had plenty of fat, in the right places so to speak, so I hung them up and made them last. Still I could not satiate. When I left their camp, I moved north, almost starving again. The first time I found safety I thought everything was going to be all right, except the food I was offered was not the food I needed to nourish me. I feasted again on the new food and then again moved on, always feasting, always moving on. I fed on so many, not enough to fill me."

Caruthers stopped walking. He seemed to be scanning the rooftop. I was confident the darkness was protecting me.

"I am sure you understand," he said. "Women are my favorite delight. But I don't believe in wasting a morsel." On that word, Caruthers busted into a dead run toward the Greenhouse and then leapt high enough up the glass wall to grip his hands onto the edge of the roof. The silhouette of his lanky body pulled up onto the roof while I stood there frozen, stunned. That he could jump to the roof hadn't occurred to me. Before he could make the walkway, I took three long strides and cast myself off the Greenhouse and onto the garage. My body slammed onto the metal roof. I tucked into a ball so I could slide down. The ground met me hard, but I rolled as best I could.

Gareth grabbed my shoulder and lifted me to my feet. He reached over to the quad and hit the ignition button. I asked, "What happened to the SUV?"

"Just get on," he urged.

I did as he said. The metal above thumped loudly. Caruthers was coming. "Can we blow this remotely?" I asked.

"That was never going to work," said Gareth. "Caruthers wants blood. Now run."

I gunned toward the gate without looking back.

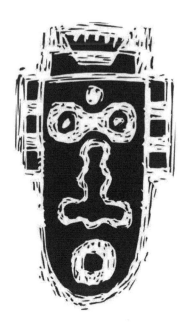

TWENTY-TWO

With the throttle wide open, the quad was across the yard in seconds. My target was the cone of light over the gate. I tried to swerve to a stop behind the concrete barrier and was thrown from the quad onto the fence. My body slammed hard, triggering the floodlight from the motion detector. Everything slipped into slow motion. My eyes fixed on the rectangle floodlight and the camera lens autofocusing on me. What felt like seconds was only an instant. Like a giant light switch had been flicked on, suddenly the dark night above the floodlight was bright as day. The fence pushed back and hung to the side before the horrendous roar of the blast thundered in my skull and that bright daylight was replaced by a hellfire blizzard of flaming debris. Chunks of what was the garage and Powerhouse ripped through the chain link. The concrete barrier to my side rocked, threatening to crush me, and then fell back.

Caruthers may have reached Gareth, but not before the natural gas and fuel containers went up.

A mountain of flame towered above the barrier. I pulled myself up. A crater filled the space where the garage and Powerhouse had been. Most everything within twenty meters of the blast had disintegrated. What little was left of the compound was burning. Two walls of the med hut still stood at the edge of the blast and farther to the side were flaming remnants of a few pods. The barracks, tool shed, and water shed farther over were all burning. The flames mostly came from debris that had pasted the sides of the walls and rooftops. Burning debris was everywhere. The Greenhouse, the only building on the other side of the crater, was essentially leveled. Jagged shards of the thick lower glass panes jutted up from odd points.

Past the crater, half a klick into the Agrofield, the stainless steel arcs of the huge pivot sprinkler cut the night horizon with the reflection of the burning compound. That time I counted the bodies. Caruthers had rehung Jenner and Hannah, and there were four more, June, Hakim, Gaz, and Max. The dangling corpses were perfectly spaced apart, the bonfire beneath dwarfed by the blaze of the compound. The brighter light made clear to me what Caruthers had been doing in those final minutes. All of the bodies were stripped of not just their clothes, but their skin.

My gut tightened. I convulsed forward. Once, then twice. At first, my throat gagged dry heaves and then acrid vomit, from somewhere way deep inside me, found a way up and spewed out two, three times, until there wasn't any more to release, and then still I wretched dryly. My lower stomach seized tight. I stayed bent forward, my hands on my knees.

My eyes watered. My skull pounded. I waited for another round that didn't come. My abs were sore, though my insides relaxed as quickly as they had erupted. My head hung low. I began to breathe in through my nose and out my mouth. The stomach acid curdled my tongue and the stench of vomit permeated my sinuses. I wiped my lips with the back of my hand and opened the last bottle of water in my lower pants pocket. I slowly raised myself and then filled my mouth with enough fluid to swish, rinse, and spit. I wiped my mouth again and raised my eyes to the blaze.

There he was, Caruthers.

Not a pile of his remains or a smear of meat that I thought must be Caruthers. No, there he was upright, over near the pods, peering right at me. I told myself that could not be him. The garage had disintegrated. Gareth had disintegrated. In Iraq, I had witnessed what had happened to soldiers that were not as close to an IED with half a blast. Even thrown, Caruthers should have been all kinds of jelly inside and out. I would have been if not for the barrier.

Caruthers was not jelly.

The heat from the fire, coursing in waves, warped my vision.

That had to be what was happening. Nothing could survive that blast. Gareth had said the heated air, in a steep thermal inversion, rapidly expanding and decreasing in density, created an optical phenomenon, an illusion, a fata morgana. Caruthers was taller than before and not as wretched. His clothes had burned away, leaving him naked, bloody, and gleaming in the light of the flames, bathed in a greasy crimson glow. The muscles he had begun to develop earlier were defined, like an athlete, a swimmer, with the leanness of an animal, a predator. His fingers were claws as long as his forearms, his lips were gone and his teeth like a normal man's, except they were ten times the length, the entirety of his jaw deformed to fit them, and he pierced me with those giant, wide open, penetrating eyes. He was teeth and eyes, big, round, bulging right in my direction. He didn't scan the yard, he didn't jerk around searching for me. He stood up from the base of that blast, turned directly toward me, and began to casually walk in my direction.

His eyes locked on me, delighted. If he had lips, I would have thought that twisted freak was smiling at me.

I didn't move. Not at first.

I watched him come closer.

The waves of heat singed my cheeks. My mouth hung open. My tongue swelled. I didn't even want to move. Caruthers, the heinous creature, had seduced me.

Caruthers was halfway across the yard before I realized I hadn't moved. The center of his glaring eyes glowed that ominous blue. The orbs flared with reflections of burning debris.

I climbed onto the quad and punched the electric start button. Compelled by a force from behind, I looked back. Caruthers was running.

I slammed the gear and squeezed the throttle. The quad flew forward over the remains of the gate, strewn loose and away from the twisted fence by the explosion, and into the darkness. The lights of the quad flooded the hard pack sand road away from Agroland. I bent my head back once and was sure that Caruthers was a step behind me. I squeezed the throttle further and swore I felt a tear and pull at the back of my shirt. I kept running full throttle into the morning, and then, far from any road or recognizable landmarks, when the quad went empty, I continued north on foot.

I had less than half a bottle of water left. I nursed that bottle so slowly. I kept moving forward in what I thought was the same direction. The desert is so much like the big lake where I grew up. In the winter, when the ice froze over and the snow would pile on, you could walk all day thinking you were in a straight line. And maybe you were, maybe not. The desert is like that.

I must have been out there for days, two, more. I was dying. I thought I was dead. No water. No water.

I was ready to tap out.

I wanted to finish, be done, my body ached everywhere and my skull was on fire. You cannot believe. Then, like an angel of mercy, he came walking toward me from the horizon, tall and dreamy. I never put that together before, two and two, the angel of mercy, the angel of death. They can be one and the same. The angel was right there, first nothing, then ripples, and then that silhouette. Then the world went blank and I woke up here in the hospital tent. Here in the refugee camp. I'm safe here. Here in the UN camp. I mean, there's what, half a million Syrians here? Caruthers can't get to me here. I am going to be okay. I am going to be okay.

* * * * *

The syringe slipped into Aker's arm, drifting him off to bliss. The young doctor tossed the dirty needle onto the bedside pan, reached over and shut off the recorder, and then clasped both hands behind his neck.

"Hey Tom, did you hear that?"

Two beds over, another doctor pulled the thread from a stich, "No nuttier than anybody else that's crawled in here over the last year. That group of refugees that came in dosed with that psychedelic aerosol had all kinds of strange to tell." He shook his head.

"Yeah," the first doctor nodded. "The Peace Keepers they sent out didn't find anyone in what was left of that compound he came from. He's either delusional or lying. They're going to take him out of here in a few days and incarcerate him until they can finish the investigation. They think he killed everybody with the blast or hauled them out to the desert. Once they find the bodies he'll stand trial."

Tom stood up and shook his head, "Twisted."

A young aid worker entered the tent, panting. He bent forward and grabbed his knees. "We found another survivor out there."

"The more the merrier," said Tom.

"You don't understand," said the young man. "This is new.

This guy shouldn't be alive. He is as fried as a chip."

The first doctor lifted his head. "Is he conscious?"

"Remarkably, and he keeps repeating, over and over, 'So many, not enough, So many, not enough'."

THE
END

ABOUT THE AUTHOR

Daniel Arthur Smith is the author of the international bestsellers THE CATHARI TREASURE, THE SOMALI DECEPTION, and a few other novels and short stories.

Raised in Michigan, he graduated from Western Michigan University where he studied philosophy and comparative religion. He has been a teacher, bartender, barista, poetry house proprietor, technologist, and a Fortune 100 consultant across North America and Europe.

Though American born, Daniel has traveled to over 300 cities in 22 countries, residing in Los Angeles, Kalamazoo, Prague, Crete, and now writes in Manhattan where he lives with his wife and young sons.

For more information, visit danielarthursmith.com

Printed in Great Britain
by Amazon

36440307R00068